Balls

Balls

a novel

JULIAN TEPPER

THIS IS A GENUINE BARNACLE BOOK.

A Barnacle Book | Rare Bird Books
453 South Spring Street, Suite 531
Los Angeles, CA 90013
abarnaclebook.com
rarebirdbooks.com

FIRST TRADE PAPERBACK EDITION

Extended Edition additional material used with permission, including: "In Which Philip Roth Gave Me Life Advice" by Julian Tepper, courtesy of the *Paris Review Daily*; "Leave Philip Roth Alone!" by Julian Tepper, courtesy of *The Daily Beast*; "Writing is easy: just open a vein" by David L. Ulin, courtesy of *Los Angeles Times*.

Library of Congress Cataloging-in-Publication Data

Tepper, Julian—
Balls: A Novel/by Julian Tepper

1. Tepper, Julian— 2. Fiction. 3. New York, NY. 4. Music—Piano. 5. Cancer.

ISBN-13: 978-0-9839255-7-6 (hardcover)
ISBN-13: 978-1-940207-03-2 (paperback)

For Jenna

ONE

Just as some people didn't discuss their past marriages, their police records, their finances and addictions, Henry Schiller didn't talk about his health. He'd told no one about the sharp pain that he'd felt in his groin over the past month. Instead, day after day, with legs hung over the bed and hands pressed to ears, Henry, a tired, stooped, pale-faced man, had insisted to himself that he was fine, that rarely ever was the body gravely sick, and he had nothing to fear. Besides, the human race was resilient. Just look at us go, still here after all this time.

A song writer, a lounge player, Henry had even penned a tune on the subject. At his piano, with his fingers coming down strong on the keys and his breathing hurried, he'd sung the chorus over and over again, in search of calm:

A thousand curious aches,
In the course of a lifetime.

Why get unsettled,
Mentally?
For the belly rails,
The brain ails,
The heart, it wails.
And you keep going.

But the song, entitled, *It's Probably Nothing*, did little to comfort him.

He was playing jazz standards three nights a week at the Beekman Hotel. Feeling well throughout the beginning of spring, by early May he was often zoning out at the keys. To some of the regulars it was obvious that he wasn't himself. One evening it was tightness in his groin which forced him to let up right in the middle of *All of Me*. The next, suffering deep emotional strain, he twice forgot his place, stopped, then started from the top. Rubbing his forehead, he would say, Oh, sorry. I can't remember where I am. He was numb, his color pale. His mind was churning. The regulars watched, expecting him to begin playing again at any minute. But instead, staring off into the shadowed corners of the room, he'd drum up more lyrics about his health.

Cringing,
From the waist up,
Ready to retch.

Or:

These are growing pains,
Still growing.

Later, slumped over his piano in his apartment on First Avenue, he would try putting the lyrics to music. Never did they amount to much. But he knew there was inspiration to be found in his condition. His life interested him less. It wasn't much of a life. He was thirty years old. Still romanticizing his heroes, he was well aware that his own, like Count Basie and Duke Ellington, had done great things by his age. Perhaps he didn't have what it took. He let opportunities pass him by. He wasn't crafty enough to get things over on people. He was once good-looking, but now he never slept. His face, with its dark bags under the eyes and wan cheeks, countenanced a man with emotional troubles. But what of these emotions? He wasn't open with others, but he knew himself well. At least he'd once thought so. His psychological map had begun redrawing itself, seemingly. With thirty years behind him, he could see he'd arrived nowhere. Certainly he was no wiser than he'd been ten or even twenty years earlier. Perhaps he'd been smartest as a young boy, he'd felt freer then. Some said he closed himself off. It was true these days he saw no friends. But what man wanted to socialize when his nipples were as sensitive as Henry's? He'd been waking in the middle of the night, disoriented by fear. Having sweated through the sheets, sickened by nerves, his mind would deliver the order:

You can't die. You can't.

He was too young, he expected to have more time. He was in fine physical shape. He was strong, his teeth were good, his vision, too. Dark hair grew thick on his head. His bones and spine were solid, his digestion was normal, his feet were large, able feet.

Through his bedroom window across gridlocked First Avenue was the United Nations, an aquamarine streak rising high towards the sky. Staring up at it in desperation, his chest would constrict and with the blood gone from his face, he'd think how he must stop denying the truth. And what was that? He'd discovered a hard pellet in his testicle. For how long had it been there? Weeks. Maybe more. It needed looking at. But he didn't want to see a doctor. He detested them. Was there anyone else he could turn to for a medical opinion? Did it have to be *one of those people?* Was he limited to that option alone? What other did he have? Should he go a holistic route? Check with an acupuncturist? Browse the aisles of a health food store? However any person in his right mind wouldn't take a chance here—and Henry had reprimanded himself for even entertaining the thought. He must see a doctor.

What about Paula? He'd said nothing to her about his health. That had to change.

You should tell her this minute.

It was a warm, rainy day in early June. Henry's appointment with Dr. Martz was scheduled for 10:00 A.M. Paula would leave with him. Her parents were in town for her graduation tomorrow, and she was meeting them at their hotel room at the Carlyle. It was nearly time to leave. Henry was going around his apartment, shutting the lights. A storm was coming. The sky was dark—it seemed like it wasn't morning yet, but the time was ten past nine. Wind rattled the screens in the tin windows. The apartment was very small, with a bedroom, a living room, a kitchen, and a bathroom. There were instruments everywhere, a tambourine in the newspaper stand next to the toilet, a recorder on the windowsill beside his bed, a triangle hung from a nail in the shower. You never knew when inspiration would strike. Below the piano in the living room was a colorful silk rug which he'd found on the curb. Biographies and mysteries, Atlases, encyclopedias filled cedar shelves on the walls. In the winter, the black tiled kitchen was ten degrees colder than the outside air, and in summer, ten degrees warmer. But the stove was big and white and resembled the hood of a 1950s Cadillac. He leaned on it with one hand, looking through the hallway at Paula in the bedroom, polishing her violin. She was using an oily beige rag. With what diligence she cleaned the instrument. She got into every crevice, every nook, under the bridge, between the knobs. She was dressed in gray tights, flats, a white blouse and maroon skirt, a more conservative outfit than she was used to, one worn especially for her father and step-mother. On her neck was a simple gold chain bought for her by Henry, a gift for her twenty-first birthday, celebrated this past March. Her black hair was wet from the shower and worn back in a tight ponytail. Under sharp dark brows—and much of Paula had a kind of sharpness, her elbows and nipples, the tip of her small nose—were large blue eyes. The brightness of these eyes was indicative of her positive outlook.

Why shouldn't she be positive? Her future looked very good. Henry was far past the point of jealousy. He understood that he didn't have her talent, her will. After two years of striving tirelessly to keep up, he'd accepted this with some relief. The person he must have been to envy Paula her dead mother, as if his own mother dying in an auto wreck when he was a boy would have made his piano sound as beautiful as Paula's violin. It frightened him to remember this. And yet back then he could still talk with confidence about writing songs for artists. *Things* were happening. He, too, was *going places.* That was no longer evident. He'd struggled for a whole year on his song about New York before giving up. Recently he'd tried his hand at jingles to make some money. The jingle hadn't sold in the end, and he'd told Paula that it had looked like it would.

In Henry's bedroom she continued to shine her violin, the instrument gleaming under the yellow overhead light. She was speaking to him of France, Germany, and Austria, how she'd probably see these places soon. After graduating, what else was there to do with her summer but go to Europe? And if she could play recitals for some men and women of influence there, people who could facilitate her passage into the higher echelons of classical music, if her professor, and ex-lover, Jeffrey Moss would keep his word and make these things happen, it would be preferred, she said. How wonderful it would be when she was out of school and really living, her violin the impetus of good times and new experiences, it was what she had always hoped would come of her efforts.

He said, Sure, Paula, yes that is great.

He hadn't been listening. His heart was beating strong inside his chest. With a warm pain there at the back of his throat, he grimaced so that his forehead became thin rolls of skin. But you have to tell her about this growth, said Henry, to himself.

In the doorway to the bedroom, Paula was plucking the strings of her violin. Only five foot four inches, with every detail about her graduation and the time to follow she seemed to grow in height. Her complexion darkened, and her mouth couldn't break with its smile so that her straight white teeth gleamed. It was apparent to Henry, in the grayness filling the apartment, that he must force the words, chuck them from his mouth, one by one. He positioned himself at the foot of the bed. The violin case was open beside him and Paula was placing the instrument back inside it. Watching her quickly shut the metal latches, he said, I have to tell you something.

What? she asked. She couldn't be blamed for her hopeful expression, Henry had disguised any sense of urgency with a cheerful tone.

He said, Paula…I…I'm having a situation.

What is it?

Kissing her knuckles, he sighed, accusing himself of cowardice.

Are you all right?

Letting go of her hand, he began to pace the room. Sweat dripped down his back. Between his eyes was a strong pain. But could he tell her? If he were going to arrive at the doctor's on time, he had to do it now.

Paula, her hand pushing back through her black hair, said, Are you going to tell me or what?

Henry replied, Yes. I'm sorry, Paula. It's...it's just my lower-back. There's a little bit of discomfort. Just a little pinching, he told her.

She said, For how long?

Not very. About a week.

Her flat chest arching, she said to him, You should see a doctor.

I'm seeing one this morning.

Good, she answered, jovially.

Henry didn't say anything more about his health. And turning off lights in the bedroom and bathroom, he reckoned that he shouldn't. He didn't know what this growth was. Why upset her before having all the information? What if it were nothing? He would have made things difficult on her for no reason.

Speak with the doctor, he told himself. This way you can be sure you aren't working her up unnecessarily.

Henry went to be examined by Dr. Philip Martz, his general practitioner of fourteen years. He rode a crowded bus to the West Side through Central Park, the stoned-in transverse flooded. Paula had left at the same time. Before parting at the corner, Henry had told her not to say a word about his back to her parents. He'd said with the graduation tomorrow and the lunch to follow, he didn't want to spend any time discussing his physical problems with Marcel and Denise Mills. Paula had said he didn't have to worry, she wouldn't tell them a word about it.

Yet even if the worst were true about his health—and moving from his seat to the bus door, Henry felt certain it was—he wouldn't let anyone know. No friends, nor family. No one. It would be much easier to deal with this alone. Besides, he didn't need help. He was strong, capable. Tough. There was nothing he himself couldn't handle. To keep his father, mother and brother from knowing wouldn't be very difficult. For twenty years his father had lived in Los Angeles, drawn there from New York by his work in television. His mother had given up her law career, remarried and now made her home, not here, but in Memphis. His brother was attending business-school in Texas. Henry was the last Schiller left in New York. The apartment was sold. There were no more Sunday dinners. Communication happened by phone or email.

But if I have to speak to them, I'll lie, thought Henry, taking a wide step off the bus over water flowing thickly along the curb. The last thing I want is for my mother or father to get on a plane and come here to help me.

He should have brought an umbrella, the rain was coming down strong. He rushed with his suit jacket pulled over his head down Central Park West into the low-lit Deco lobby of the Century Apartments. He didn't wait for the heavily stooped doorman to admit him but said Doctor Martz's name aloud and proceeded quickly through the double-wide doors. His heart felt pierced through, enervated. His head ached. In the damp, crowded waiting area, he sat with full awareness of the growth there in his scrotum. He thought he could even feel it. Perhaps it was better to stand.

Near the front door, he found a place, but kept closing his legs at the thighs, feeling the growth against the fabric of his underwear. He had the idea that he should laugh. Because this was preposterous. That this was anything serious was the creation of a delusional man. He was fine. He felt a bit sluggish, sure, and his right knee had been *popping* all morning. But so what? He wondered whether he should leave. He could keep an eye on the problem and if it worsened over time, he'd come back and have it looked at. So it was settled, that was it, he wasn't staying.

He prepared to walk out. But his name was called and before Henry knew it, a nurse was escorting him into a small examination room. She told him to remove everything but his underwear. Having known the doctor a long time, he didn't mind letting him think he was succeeding at life. For that reason he'd worn his tan suit this morning, the finest he owned, a black gingham shirt and powder blue tie. He hung the jacket on the back of a chair in the corner, and the pants were folded and placed neatly on the seat. Undressed, he observed himself in a mirror. He looked thinner than usual. Paler, too. He was certain the fluorescents had something to do with it. This lighting was selected to make him appear particularly unwell. What other way was there to see it? They were clever businessmen, these doctors. But telling Paula his back ailed him was as good a lie as any. With the inevitable bad posture that came with sitting at a piano, in time you did yourself in, a pinched nerve got you, a slipped disc. You had to sit up straight and more importantly strengthen your back muscles. Henry had complained for months how he had to stop slacking off and do pushups and sit-ups as he once had every day. He might start right away, on the blue linoleum. But the floor looked cold.

And here was the doctor. Oh, Martz looked terrific. Had he just come from the Caribbean? His tan was even across his face. Handsome, relaxed, he was in his mid-40s, of average height, his shoulders a comfortable width apart. He had clear blue eyes, a widow's peak. With efficient strokes he filled out a patient's charts, the sound of his pen jotting sharp in Henry's ear.

How's your mother? In Memphis, right?

Yes. She's doing fine, doctor.

And your brother?

Fine, said Henry. They're all fine.

He couldn't discuss family. Not now. Seated with his black hairy legs dangling from the examination table, he took a quick breath, drew in his shoulders. He wondered if he should lie to the doctor about why he'd come today. Tell him he was dizzy or seeing gray? It wouldn't have been the first time the doctor had heard him complain of these symptoms. He could ask for a Valium prescription. Wasn't that all he needed, something to loosen him up? But he reminded himself that if the growth were nothing, some burst blood vessel, he could leave here a free man. And why not risk that?

Holding his hands out to Martz, supplicatingly, he told him, Doc, listen, I…I found a growth…on my testicle.

A *growth?* said Martz. The doctor quit writing at once and dispensed with his clipboard.

Yes, Henry told him. About the size of pea and solid hard.

Which testicle is it?

The left.

Lower your underpants. Lower them. Come on, Martz half-shouted.

Henry did as he was told, but his hands were shaking, his throat was suddenly dry and Martz, himself, seemed genuinely agitated watching Henry recline onto the table. Without delay the doctor's gloved hand seized Henry's crotch. The digging of his fingers made Henry nauseous.

Where is it? he asked. Is it *here?*

A little lower, said Henry, turning his face to the wall. At the far end of the table his right foot trembled.

Martz was drawing Henry's scrotum one way and back the other. He did it a half-dozen times. Henry had had many physicals performed right here. During any one of them the doctor had spent between ten and twenty seconds inspecting his testicles. But Martz had never treated them this aggressively. He was yanking on the skin, forcing the testes in every which direction.

At last he said, *Mmmmmm.*

You've found it?

I've found something.

Henry peered down at his sideward bending penis in all that black hair, ready to cry. He said, What is it?

Between the brown examination table and hazardous material box and jars of syringes, Martz pulled off his gloves. He didn't answer Henry's question, but told him to dress. Anxiously rubbing his mouth with thumb and forefinger he remained silent, his light eyes flickering, his face tense and searching. He said, Henry, I want you to listen to me. I'm not going to tell you to worry just yet.

You're not?

No. I want to give a call over to Dr. Glen Dahl. He's a urologist on East 74th Street. You'll see him today.

I'll go there this minute?

Exactly.

Martz placed his hand firmly on Henry's shoulder. Staring into his patient's eyes, he said, We don't know what this is. It could be nothing. So please, Henry, try and be calm.

Try and be calm? said Henry, to himself. But how?

It was forty minutes later and he was in his second examination room of the day, this one at the Park Avenue offices of Dr. Glen Dahl. In a blue gown left open at the back he paced the cool, metallic room. The air conditioning was degrees colder here than at Martz's and Henry, still damp from the rain, was shivering. He had arrived by taxi. But on the way over he'd already begun to feel that he was being had. These doctors were using fear to ensnare him. He was their victim, he and *others.* They threw you into these trials and what could you do but follow their orders, paying at each stop along the way. Thank god for George. His father's brother owned a car dealership up in Yonkers. Three year ago he'd put Henry on payroll so as to provide him with medical insurance (albeit illegally). Henry couldn't afford to be here otherwise.

The room was small and gloomy, and the furniture—an examination table, a wooden coat stand, a red felt upholstered chair and metal file cabinet—struck him as old. The mahogany cupboard storing medical supplies was also an outdated model. But where had Martz sent him? Who was this doctor that couldn't keep up with the times and present the newest designs? His lips fluttering, Henry's attention shifted to the medical literature tacked to the walls. His hand on his brow, as if anticipating pain there, he began to read about infections of the epididymis, torsions of the testicle, the TSE:

TESTICULAR SELF-EXAMINATION:

1. Place thumb atop testicle; the index and middle fingers below.
2. Roll the testicle back and forth.
3. Be aware of any changes to your testicle, of size or shape, or if any lumps or swelling have occurred.
4. A healthy testicle is egg-shaped, firm, yet smooth.
5. Lastly, check the epididymis, attached to the top and back of the testicle. It's tube-like in shape. Be aware of any changes to the epididymis.

Be aware of any *what?*

Terrified, he said, But I can't do it. I can't.

Then he heard behind him the metal click of the door, and jumped—there was Dr. Dahl coming forward to shake his hand.

Henry Schiller?

Yes, he said.

You were sent here by Martz?

I was.

Wasting no time, Henry explained to Dahl that he'd found a growth on his testicle. The doctor, nodding his head, asked Henry how long ago this was.

A couple weeks, said Henry.

Okay.

But I could be wrong. It might have been longer. I mean, I don't know.

All right. Don't worry, Henry.

Dr. Dahl was in his late sixties and appeared in good health. Tall, thin and strong, with a wide forehead which rose above thick eyebrows, he could give up urology today and go into commercials. His honest face and full head of gray hair would sell drugs for enlarged prostates and erectile dysfunction, diet drinks, golf magazines, multivitamins, too. But that didn't mean Henry would lay back and let himself be taken advantage of. Not a chance, said Henry, to himself. He was ready to defend against any ploys. The doctor asked him to stand up straight. Henry did as he was told. With his right hand Dahl started to walk his fingers across the surface of Henry's testicles. Unlike Martz, Dahl didn't wear a glove. His fingers were cold, the tips coarse. He apologized before squeezing, he knew this was unpleasant, it had to be done.

I understand, said Henry. I'm okay.

However, he was losing the strength to stay up, and to himself he was saying, Oh, fuck me, god.

Dahl continued to feel about Henry's left testicle. He was slow and delicate, precise. After another twenty seconds, in the doctor's eyes appeared a look of grim discovery. Henry caught it, and asked if everything was all right. Dahl didn't say, but instructed him to lie down on the padded table.

We're almost done here, he told Henry. Just hang on.

Feeling the doctor's long fingers seize the tumor, Henry swallowed hard. His mood swung lower. Measuring his tone for spite—in his vulnerable position, he didn't want to come off rude and offend the man—he said, So, how is it, doctor?

Dahl wasn't finished, the tumor was still between his fingers and he was applying pressure there, his face close to Henry's testicles.

Is it very bad? said Henry.

The doctor was touching Henry's forearm with his free hand. His fingers held him tightly there, to the point of pain. He then released Henry's testicles. With lips pursed, he looked blankly at the patient, not saying anything. Finally, he told him, I want you to dress and meet me in my office. Take your time.

Your office? Dr. Dahl, whatever this is, you can tell me here.

Yet Dahl said, Henry, just come next door to my office, and he left the room.

A minute later Henry was seated at a large glass desk looking out through a window facing Park Avenue where the rain still came down hard. Positioned across from him in a brown leather chair was Dahl. The warm, sympathetic voice he was using to explain the likeliness that Henry had cancer of the testicles could not be taught at college. This was real compassion. Henry thought so. But what was this next part about? He would have to undergo a scrotal ultrasound? If a tumor were discovered, blood work and radiography would be used to determine the stage of the cancer? The rest would be known once pathology results on the testicle came in?

Dahl was apologizing. I really am sorry, Henry. Do you want to take a moment?

But Henry, numb from the shoulders down, was unable to speak. There was a low buzzing in his head. He felt tightness in his throat, his groin. Looking up at the doctor, trying to answer him, he choked back his words. At last, what came out was:

Just tell me what I do?—and he coughed so that his shoulders curled inward.

Dahl said, If the ultrasound shows that it *is* cancer, we'll have to perform an orchiectomy.

Which means *what?*

It means that the testicle would be removed, Henry.

For good? he cried.

Yes, for good.

Henry's head slumped forward. With a pleading look he asked why the doctor couldn't just clean the testicle and put it back where he found it.

No, I'm sorry to say we don't do that, Henry.

Why *not?* he shouted.

Dahl crossed his arms, and gazing sadly at Henry, he said, Because the testicle is not good anymore.

Leaning forward between his knees, Henry let out a scream. Dahl got up, offering him water. But Henry said no, he didn't want to drink anything. He was fine.

I'm fine, he said. Though he looked like he might faint, and his eyes were closing. So what, you're saying my testicle is gone—*gone* for good?

If the ultrasound shows signs of a cancerous tumor, I'm afraid so, Dahl said. I'm very sorry, Henry. I'm really very sorry.

Oh—*fuck*.

His large hands patting down the air around him, the doctor said, I have to tell you quite often, Henry, *Henry* quite often, depending on the stage of the cancer, recovery happens at a very, very high rate. Which is good news. You'll still have your life.

But why couldn't I have never been born in the first place? said Henry, to himself. He slapped his hands to the table, standing. I can't believe it, he said. I knew it was going to be cancer, I did. But to hear you say it, it's just, it's—

Do you need a moment? the doctor asked again.

No, I'm fine, I'm fine. He returned to his chair. The doctor was speaking, but Henry, collapsing mentally, couldn't hear him. He interrupted Dahl, blurted out:

What about sex?

The doctor said, Henry, in most circumstances the healthy testicle compensates with good results. Likely you'll still be able to produce sperm and sexually little if any changes will occur. This will all depend on a few specifics, for instance, the stage of the cancer, whether it's been caught early and can be treated without chemotherapy, as well as a whole list of variables that we shouldn't get swept up in now. But I'm sure you'll be able to have many, *many*, children.

Many children? said Henry.

Here, Dahl told him they shouldn't get too far ahead of themselves. Let's see what the ultrasound looks like. We'll set up an appointment for tomorrow morning.

Henry gave the doctor a strange look with the eyes unfocused and the mouth stretched wide. He said, I have to be at my girlfriend's graduation at ten. I can't miss it.

You might have to.

Henry told Dahl he'd rather postpone the ultrasound than not be at Paula's graduation.

Postpone? Dahl said he was risking his life with every day he waited. I'm sure your girlfriend will understand.

Can you schedule the ultrasound for early in the morning?

I could try.

It's very important I be there. This is a special time in a person's life.

Dahl, nonplussed, said, I'll see what I can do. I can't make any promises. But you need to have that ultrasound, Henry.

I will.

Tomorrow.

Tomorrow, Henry assured him.

So children. Many children. That was the purpose of his testicles—to give life. However, Nature was pulling him out of the pool, giving him a tap on the shoulder, saying, YOU. Not your sperm. Grab a towel and get on the side.

Henry, stumbling with a half-broken mind from Dahl's office out onto Park Avenue, knew this had to do with more than just reproduction, though. This, he shuddered, is a matter of life and death.

Besides, as far as reproduction went, Nature didn't work that way. Or did She? *Did She?* But how did Nature work when she worked like *this*? And was it Nature that had done this to him, or, was it something else? Something I did in the past to harm myself?

The rain had stopped and Henry looked south to the top of the MetLife Building where the sun poking through white clouds shone bright. In the path of a warm June breeze he recalled a time when the MetLife sign had read PANAM and he was young, healthy, mischievous, free. He could plead and protest with a great freedom of mind, he could fantasize about the impossible, he could even fear God.

But what did I do? said Henry, to himself. How did I ruin my testicle?

Thinking back through the apartments in which he'd lived, those uptown and downtown, on the East Side and West, on no block did he see a power plant or chemical refinery, a garbage facility or telephone company which might have housed cancer-giving toxins. He ate well, lots of fruits and vegetables, drank moderately, smoked only on rare occasions. His coffee intake could be very high. But what did that mean about his testicles? Perhaps this was the result of stress.

It was true, six years ago, in the autumn of 2004, Henry did begin to suffer an odd condition. He didn't feel right, he was off, his equilibrium askew, his vision gray. He saw the world as if a filter had been slipped over his eyes. He thought he was dying, but he went to doctors and they told him he was fine, a strong and healthy young man. Try not eating salt, suggested one neurologist, it could be that you have high blood pressure. For three months Henry hardly ingested salt. His state didn't improve. (He could kill that doctor.) But he let another doctor scan his brain and yet another peer into his ears, his chest and liver, too. Nothing explained his symptoms. An ophthalmologist outfitted him in a pair of wire-rimmed specs, but the dizziness persisted. Because his vision was fine, the world was *in* focus, it was the color, the tint and vibrancy which appeared unlike it had in his first twenty-four years of life.

He was earning money teaching piano to children, but he could barely get through a lesson. The filter strained his energies. At home his writing was suffering. Fragmented parts which he couldn't expand into whole songs, he had more of these than he knew what to do with. For the first time ever his mind was too clouded to make sense out of notes. His frustration mounted. It became too painful to sit at the piano. He even covered the instrument in a white tablecloth, the sight of it was cutting away at whatever good judgment remained in him. He began to think and behave in other odd ways, too. For instance, he'd written in black marker on his refrigerator a statement about his body, that it must be functioning according to its age:

For why did I ever think that I'd feel physically well through my twenties when a time existed not long ago in the long history of humankind when thirty—not eighty—was considered old age?

Why wouldn't I be breaking down at twenty-four? This is normal. The body changes. It weakens. It chips. It fractures and fails. Don't fret. Don't cry about it. But accept and move on. This is life.

Every day Henry feasted on new platitudes, and for a while he bought into them, too. Along the edge of his desk he'd scrawled in blue ink:

Visual filters are a physical reality faced by all people everywhere. No two people see the world alike. We all have our own filter. And mine is gray in tone. So there it is.

One rationale after another refracted through him until his second year of dizziness when he descended further into depression. His piano remained covered in a sheet. He'd stopped giving lessons and was working concession at a movie theater downtown. The fear of spending the rest of his life in a vertiginous state had him considering suicide. To live sixty more years perhaps, just like this.

I'll never make it, thought Henry.

Riding the subway one afternoon he ran into an old friend, Whitney Shields, the clarinetist. Whitney was twice Henry's age. The nose on his tender face was long and narrow with a complex, ridged tip. His large brown eyes were full of knowledge. At the sight of him, Henry's guard lowered and he told Whitney about his dizziness.

Brother, he said, to Henry, it sounds to me like you need help.

You're probably right. It's hard for me to admit, but I think I *do*.

You ever tried a shrink?

I haven't.

I tell you, they've pulled me out of a few slumps.

Henry called Martz to ask for a referral. He suggested a psychiatrist, Penelope Andrews, on the West Side. Martz didn't know her personally, but had heard good things. Henry contacted her at once. Just minutes into their conversation, in a soft, unhurried tone, she'd told him he sounded troubled. Henry had felt grossly misjudged. How could she know so much about him? Was she a psychiatrist or a psychic? He considered canceling his appointment. But desperate to feel better, he showed up at the scheduled time. Indeed, many of the doubts he'd had about coming were soon quashed by the doctor's long, smooth, un-stockinged legs which crossed before him during their first session. She wore a short dress of a kind of powder blue color. Hers was a full bosom and she had the sort of fleshy stomach which made Henry want to grab on. Brown wavy hair hung past her shoulders. Greeting him at the door to her office on West 81st Street, her mouth, full and red, had smiled at Henry.

He'd said, Nice to meet you, doctor.

And she'd told him, Please, call me Penelope.

Before sitting Henry had looked around the room. Would he be open with his thoughts here? The brown wall to wall carpeting was oppressive. The drawn curtains sealed them into a semi-darkness, which affected him like a soporific. The dark wood shelves and thick medical volumes were stifling. He found a number of things to complain about. But sitting across from Dr. Andrews, his energy, his spirit, returned. Oh, she was something to look at. She was beautiful.

During the first half-hour Henry spoke about his condition, when it began, why he believed it had. He told her of his struggles with music. But he wanted her to talk. He knew his own thoughts, and was tired of them. However, not until the end of the session did she say much of anything. With Henry's throat dry from speech, in the sleep-inducing light, Dr. Andrews, who had exceptional calves, gazed sideways at her patient and said to him:

Henry, you remind me of a man who came to see me about a month after 9/11. He was maybe ten years older than you. He'd worked in the north tower. Or was it the south? She touched her forefinger to her lips and said, I don't remember. But the first things he complained of were symptoms just like those you're describing: Dizziness. Filter. Exhaustion. Trouble working. Depression. I diagnosed him with Post-Traumatic Stress Disorder. He'd been through something which had shocked his whole system: Getting out of that building alive, losing friends, watching it all happen again and again on the television—he fell apart. But I'm left to wonder, Henry...were you here on 9/11?

Henry's neck lengthened, his eyes shut. He wasn't sure how any of this was relevant. But he was not the expert. Shifting forward in his chair, he said:

I was on my roof. I'd been living downtown.

Did you see the towers fall?

I did.

And how did you feel afterwards?

How did I feel? Like anyone else, said Henry, I suppose I was shocked, afraid.

She said, *Right*, then wrote something on her yellow pad. Tell me, did you experience any loss of appetite?

No.

Libido?

I can't say.

Were you alone when it happened?

I was, doctor.

All alone?

There were others on my roof.

Friends?

Henry gave her a cross look. As much as any neighbor in New York is a friend. I guess we did *talk* to each other.

But otherwise you were alone?

I was.

A mournful expression on her face, she leaned forward in her chair and said, I'm sorry, Henry Schiller. I am so, so sorry. It must have been *so* hard to be by yourself that day.

Henry said nothing. He had no answer in mind.

The doctor was talking again. She was saying, The man I described for you, Henry, you should know, I fixed him. I made him better.

That's what I want, doctor. I can't tell you how bad this dizziness has been for me. I've never gone this long without playing piano. I can't remember the last time I've had anything but a one-night stand. I've fallen out of contact with my friends. I'm lost.

The doctor frowned, in earnest. She said, Well, I *want* to help you, Henry.

Thank you, doctor.

I'm going to help you.

Good. Good.

You said you were on your roof, all alone...what happened next?

Henry left Dr. Andrews' office that day in a state of extreme ambivalence. On the one hand, he didn't see how meeting once a week for forty-five minutes to discuss the events of 9/11 would improve his equilibrium or restore the confidence he'd lost in his songwriting. On the other, the doctor smelled so good, some perfume she wore, a faint orange aroma that turned him on in a way no woman had for years, and when deciding whether or not to see her again he couldn't help but imagine her heavy bosom and smooth knees—he became erect. They were scheduled to meet the following Thursday afternoon. Henry showed ten minutes early. Dr. Andrews began the session by explaining how her methods of treating 9/11 victims were somewhat untraditional. But Henry, mesmerized by the sultry tone of her voice, didn't hear her description. Nor did he ask her to repeat herself. They spent the time watching cable news, the doctor studying Henry's reactions to any mention of Iraq and Afghanistan. The next week they went to visit the World Trade Center site. Henry followed the doctor's instructions, staring long and hard at the building's footprint and like the Surrealists speaking aloud those words, any words, which came to mind:

Landscape. Cabbage. Breast. Future. Muffled. Face. Disturb. Exist. Eyeballs. Blisters. Partner. Gray. Despair. Entombed. Influx. Clasp. You. Lidless. Lizards.

That's good, Henry. That's very good.

Really?

Oh sure, Henry. You're doing splendidly.

He valued her encourgament. But then these days, whether staring at *CNN* or the WTC, Dr. Andrews didn't mind when he touched her arm or placed his hand on the small of her back. She didn't protest when he hugged her goodbye, pulling her tight against his body. She said nothing when he complimented her beauty. At times he thought he'd pay even more for her services.

That opportunity did soon arise.

The doctor said she was dissatisfied with their progress. Henry was still dizzy, depressed and closed-off musically. She proposed he start coming twice-a-week. Knowing her rates were high for him, she offered him a special price: two sessions, $300.

Take a minute, Henry. Think it over.

But Henry, breathing in that profoundly erotic mandarin aroma, told her he didn't need time. Yes, was his answer.

Yes.

He started seeing the doctor Tuesday and Thursday afternoons. Though finding no improvement in his symptoms, his fantasies about Andrews were becoming more regular. At night he closed his eyes, imagining her naked breasts, her ass. In the morning, they occupied his mind again. Enveloped by thoughts of her legs, he missed his stop on the subway. On the street he saw women with similar hair and build and followed them for blocks, thinking they might be her. He couldn't recall the last time a woman had taken possession of him like this. Perhaps he should stop seeing the doctor. Could this be *healthy?* He knew it wasn't. But he couldn't bring himself to tell Andrews it was over. He looked forward to their time together more than anything else during the week. He wouldn't give it up. He considered discussing these feelings with her. Why not? She'd told him many times that he could tell her anything.

In fact, one day Dr. Andrews, seated with her silken legs crossed and her hands folded under her chin, raised the subject herself.

Henry, she began, there's something I've been meaning to discuss with you.

The pulse at the sides of his head increased. He could hear its heavy thumping in his ear. He didn't move.

Andrews, glancing from him to the floor, drew her fingers up her long, supple neck. She said to him, I've had patients fall in love with me before, and, as difficult as that can be, I don't think it has to mean the end of our work together. We have to talk about it, though. We have to figure out what's happened.

Andrews placed her notepad under the chair, as if to tell Henry that this was not a patient-doctor matter.

Is that really what you think, said Henry, that I'm in love with you?

Dr. Andrews, bringing her hands over her lovely round knees, said, It's clear to me that this is precisely the case. You have nothing to feel ashamed of, Henry. You're a young man. You come here twice a week to unburden yourself to me, a woman some ten years your senior, and have the chance to speak your mind in ways you can't with any other person. Dependencies do develop. It's no surprise that you'd try and keep me close through sexual relations. *Henry*, she said, flashing her smile, I've sat with you for months. I know what's going on.

It's true you're such a beautiful woman, Penelope.

Mmm-hmm, she nodded her head. You've said so before.

I've thought about you *intimately* since the moment I met you.

I know you have, Henry.

Until now, Andrews had maintained a serene look on her face. But folding her arms under her chest and staring at Henry with commanding eyes, her expression became serious. She explained how she'd never once had intercourse (that was *her* word) with a patient and that she wouldn't begin now. She said her practice was her life, it meant everything to her. If only Henry knew how hard she'd worked to get here, she could never jeopardize her place in the field of psychiatry, not for anything. Her mind told her it couldn't happen. Her mind said no.

But my body, Henry...my *body* tells me something different.

And if Henry were interested in pursuing a meaningful relationship, she might open her ear and listen to what her body had asked of her, of *him*, ever since he first walked through her door.

Henry wanted to jump her right there. The doctor sensed this.

Not yet, she said.

When?

Soon. Very soon, Henry.

They met two evenings later at a restaurant in Chinatown. Henry showed first. When the doctor arrived she kissed him on the mouth before sitting. Long and hard, the kiss—their first—made clear to him he could have her whenever he was ready. However, after returning to the doctor's apartment and having sex, right away Henry wondered if he hadn't made a mistake. Something about her didn't sit right with him. In bed she was clearly very experienced, her impulses were good, he could let himself go and be taken fully in the moment.

With their bodies enfolded under the covers and the large white disk of the moon facing down at them through a window, she said:

Henry, you have so much inside you that needs to come out. I want to help you. That hasn't changed. Okay, Henry? Are you awake? Did you hear me?

Yes. I am. I heard you, he said.

His body was stiff under the covers, his heart filled with dread.

In the morning, after making love, Henry walked Andrews to work. On any street corner while awaiting the light, the doctor kissed Henry, and her hands held him powerfully at the waist. She asked if he'd cook dinner that evening. He said he would. The rest of the day was spent aggravating over how to cancel—something which he failed to do. Neither did he buy food to prepare. Nevertheless, having arrived at his apartment and learned the fate of their dinner, the doctor said she wasn't even hungry. She told him to make love to her. When they finished, she asked him:

Did you like that?

I...*yes*...I did.

I thought about you all day.

Is that true?

It is, Henry. And did you think about me?

Yes, he answered.

At least twenty times he'd meant to pick up the phone and tell her he couldn't make it. But there was no point in saying this.

There's a meeting of the World Psychiatric League in Phoenix next week. I want you to come with me.

Henry waited a moment before speaking. He told himself to say no, he couldn't go away with Andrews, that was impossible. He didn't want to. He wouldn't.

If it's a matter of money, Henry, I'll buy your ticket.

Money *is* tight.

He thought of all he had paid her. He'd never let her know it had ruined him financially.

He said, I couldn't accept. That would be too generous.

Too generous?

I think so.

The next day the doctor surprised Henry with a plane ticket. He couldn't believe it. How could she! His shock quickly led to an argument, their first. She accused him of not being honest with her. And why he couldn't be that, she didn't know. Was he a coward? Was he not a man? Was that it?

It was early evening and Henry had just arrived at the doctor's, ready to take her to dinner. But the doctor locked herself away in the bedroom and stayed there for thirty minutes. When she finally emerged, she ran straight out the apartment, disappearing for another hour. Henry waited for her to come back. He felt terrible, she was right, he was lying, he was a coward, he didn't have the guts to tell her that they shouldn't see each other anymore. Why that was true, he didn't know. If he were to theorize, as the doctor had about his emotions for over seven months, he might say it was because she was fragile, a needy person, one who latched on tight. He didn't want to hurt her. When she returned to the apartment he saw no way to tell her any of that. She was even angrier. By the time Henry had calmed her down, it was two in the morning. She told him he was no longer invited to Phoenix. She didn't want his company. She'd rather be alone.

Henry, soul-worn and dizzy, could hardly believe it himself. There he was, on his knees and saying, But I want to go with you.

No you don't. You're lying, Henry.

I'm not *lying*.

You are. You don't mean it.

I *do*.

Then look me in the eye, Henry, and tell me you want to come with me.

And for some reason Henry did look her in the eye and tell her this.

She said, You really do?

Yes, Penelope.

Really?

I want to go away with you, he said.

Now, despite Henry's lying, it remained a good trip. On the plane home from Phoenix with the doctor asleep on his shoulder he even wondered if he wasn't falling for her. He could admit to a sort of new, amorous feeling growing inside him. It had been a while since he'd heard her speak the words 9/11. There'd been no talk of the Taliban, all of that seemed done, over, in the past. That pleased Henry. He was still dizzy, his filter unchanged, his music dormant. But the doctor's idiosyncrasies, her penchant for repeating the same stories, her fear of drinking New York City tap water, rather than annoy him, were coming across as charming. Their sex life was becoming more satisfying, too. It was true, he was growing fond of her.

Then two months later the bombs exploded in the London underground, also tearing apart one double-decker bus, and Andrews called Henry to her office. He found her there as he had on so many days, seated in her chair in a short white dress. Her eyes were dark but the intensity of their look was magnified by a streak of black liner at the corner of the lids. Her mouth was sternly composed. She told him to sit. She was so worried about him, she feared the day's tragedy would derail his progress. How was he? Any dizzier? How was his filter? Grayer? Darker?

Do you want to talk about anything...anything you're feeling after this morning's events?

Not at all, he answered. But he thought terrorism was in their past. Why are we talking about this?

Because this is important, Henry. Realize, new attacks on our cities open old wounds. It wouldn't surprise me if you feel terrible.

Andrews looked at him in a posture of serious consideration. Her chin rested between her fingers, the middle and fore of the left hand, which formed a *V*. Her eyes squinted, her lips curled. Henry, she said, I think the wisest decision would be to stop having intercourse for the time being.

Excuse me?

To discontinue intercourse.

What? Why? What are you talking about?

The doctor explained how it would be wrong to reward his psychological pain with any sexual pleasure in the aftermath of the attack. It would teach his mind to link the good of sex with the horror of terrorism.

Do you understand what I'm saying, Henry?

I don't. Not even a little.

When the shock of London dies down, we'll start to do it again. I promise.

How long are you thinking, Penelope?

Three weeks max.

Three?

She came forward and embraced him. I'm here for you, she said. I will help you through this.

Celibacy was a new kind of torment, but the doctor insisted on it. She cared about Henry, and refused to do irreversible damage to his mind's sexual memory. This was her priority. Henry would live a long life, have intercourse another fifty years perhaps, she would protect him. Henry didn't know what to think. Increasingly fervent about these opinions, Andrews no longer permitted him to see her change out of her clothes, she wore jeans to sleep, she wouldn't kiss him, wouldn't touch him. She became less warm, in general. Since the start of his dizziness, he'd yet to feel this weak, confused, distracted, timid. Some part of him became afraid to be seen by the doctor. What would she make of this person? How could she respect him? And yet he couldn't stay away. When she beckoned, he went to her. He was always available, ready to accommodate Andrews, canceling plans with friends at the last minute or walking out of movies he'd gone to see alone. In his chest was a murky heat that didn't subside, even when they were together. People understood him less, for he was mumbling most of his words. At the end of three weeks, Andrews told him that he must wait a little longer. She didn't give him a date. Not wanting to make her unhappy and perhaps lose her, he told the doctor that whatever she thought was best, that's what he'd do. The sheet was off his piano. It had been for weeks, a suggestion of the doctor's. Only once had he tried to play. In the back of his mind was the feeling that perhaps he'd write a song. Sadly, the keys had never felt this unusual to the touch. He couldn't remember the notes ever sounding so foreign. Was he still a musician? Had he grown out of it? This could happen, he imagined. Why not? But if he wasn't a musician, what was he? Who was he? What did he mean to make of himself? his life? He threw the sheet back on the piano, and went to the bar.

One evening, during the second month of celibacy, Henry, picking the doctor up at work, stepped inside her office and saw that she'd been crying. Sitting down in the chair across from her, he asked the doctor what was wrong. (He really did want to know.) At first she was silent. Pressing her hands to her cheeks, she regained control of herself and told Henry:

We need to talk.

His black brow knitted, he was ready for it: she would tell him she couldn't see him anymore. There was another man. He almost stood and went straight from the room, he didn't want to hear any of it. She began to say something different, though. What she told him was that amid so much talk of terrorism, she'd never once asked him something very important:

Why was it so hard for him to accept help when he needed it? Why did he want to face all of life's difficulties on his own? Didn't he find it better having someone there, someone who understood him?

His shoulders were set back against the chair, his face perspiring. It seemed for the first time ever the doctor had said something true about his character. It *was* difficult for him to accept help. Why? Because a man made it through life alone. He took care of himself. He helped others, but never accepted handouts. That was the basis on which he remained *a man*.

Henry looked long into the doctor's eyes. He could feel his heart swelling. He choked back tears. He said, Do you feel so strongly about me, Penelope?

His question caused her to smile. I do, she said.

Why? he asked her.

She shrugged. I guess it's because I love you, Henry. Beginning to laugh, she said, I do. I love you, Henry. Do you love me? Honestly, Henry, do you?

He didn't know what to call these strong, complex emotions fixed inside his heart. But he said, Yes, I love you, Penelope.

The doctor slept with him at once, on the office floor. To be back inside her seemed like bliss.

Life continued as it had before the strike on London. Then one morning, a month later, before leaving Andrews' apartment, Henry went to the bathroom where the doctor had a whole pharmacy stocked inside the medicine cabinet—hundreds of samples given to her by the pharmaceutical companies—and to satisfy his curiosity he took a single 10mg pill of Valium which he'd been eyeing for a long while. Shortly after, heading into the subway at Verdi Square, it occurred to Henry that something was very wrong. He didn't feel right. He was off, more so than usual. Wasn't he? Leaning against the railed entrance to the subway he tried making sense of the feeling. He'd spent so much time in the past two years assessing the qualities of his condition, every slight change to his equilibrium, any difference in the shade of the filter. But what was this? *What was this?* Had his dizziness abated? Had the filter lifted? He didn't believe it. What was happening? It couldn't be. He would not accept it.

Impossible.

He didn't head straight down into the subway but ran his own series of tests, first walking back and forth along the curb. He did it with eyes opened, then closed. There was none of the usual see-sawing in his head. He looked upwards and after much gazing and consideration he decided the sky appeared the way it had in his pre-filter days: *blue.* He felt too good to go to work, he was again teaching piano to children, and he called Andrews from Central Park. He described his feeling to her: like Superman, he said.

All the weight has lifted. I can't believe it. I don't know what to do with myself.

The doctor let out a full sigh. She said, Good for you, Henry.

Good for *me?*

Henry, I have to go. I have a patient.

What?

I *have* a patient *walking* into my office.

I'm telling you I'm healed.

And I'm happy for you. I can't talk. She hung up.

Henry was sick with rage. Ready to beat down her office door, he went straight to 81st Street. She made him leave. He was being irresponsible. She was in a session. She couldn't talk. Later. Later.

Yet later she made excuses why she couldn't see him. She wasn't feeling well. She had a meeting. She had to be up early in the morning.

Henry, I have to go. Goodbye.

Henry didn't understand. Why was she shutting him out? His anguish was powerful. And yet he didn't want to cede room in his heart to misery. That's all there'd been for years. No—he wanted to celebrate his balance. He called Foster, the drummer, Greenwald, the trumpeter, Bishop, the bassist. There'd been a time when they'd often played together. They met that evening after ten p.m. in a small brick room in a warehouse in the West 40s. For the first time in years, Henry did arrive at that combination of notes and good rhythm to hit on what is sometimes called *the sweet-spot*, at times, *the nerve*, releasing a powerful surge of adrenaline into the bloodstream. The most wonderful feeling, the *best* feeling, Henry had once thought his life's purpose was to pursue it and *it* alone. Days afterwards he still felt high. The doctor still refused to see him. Therefore, he could get no more Valium. Regardless, his dizziness remained in abeyance. The filter, too, was gone. (Fixed over the eyes of another man, perhaps.) About this Henry conceived a theory and posted it on his fridge:

I only had to know something was out there which could cure me in order to stay cured. That's it. Nothing more.

He felt stronger than ever. He was eager to write music.

It was now that he began work on *All the Crazies Love Me*. A rare moment in the long haul of creation, the song, a three minute and twelve second jazz number, asked for no great labor. Henry wrote it in a single afternoon. The lyrics, which told the story of Dr. Andrews, were finished the following morning. He thought nothing of the composition. Certainly he had no idea it would become his first song to play on the radio. But eating a nova sandwich at Barney Greengrass the following week, Henry bumped into his old classmate, Zachary Walbaum. A short man, Walbaum had a terrible suffering look to him. It had been true of him even as a child. His cheeks were sunken, his face ghostly, his black hair a thinning bush with sight lines to the scalp. His large nose crumbled at the bridge. When he saw Henry, blood temporarily rushed to his head, fading a moment later.

Henry Schiller!

Walbaum had stunned Henry by kissing him on the face before taking the seat opposite him.

You look absolutely fantastic. I mean, fan-*tastic.*

Henry had known Walbaum when he was shy, quiet, morose. Now things were different. Walbaum had signed a multi-platinum selling artist and made VP at Brass Records. He had a tremendous office overlooking Fifth Avenue on 56th Street. After ordering himself a coffee and babka muffin he began explaining to Henry how it was here, in this very dining room, where anyone who was anyone in the music industry came to eat nova or sturgeon on a bagel.

And I'm not just talking about myself. Lots of industry insiders.

He started pointing around the room. That tall fella with the short gray hair was a big *macha*. And that one in the corner ran the show over at Hi-Delphi Records. Arnold Kleinfeldt, himself, the CEO at Brass, would surely be in within the hour and who knew who'd be with him. Henry admitted that he was a songwriter. Walbaum slammed his hands on the table.

Baby, I've got to hear your latest.

Henry hadn't expected to be taken so seriously. Tentative, he said, I finished a song just the other day.

You'll get it to me, *pronto.*

Henry brought a demo of *All the Crazies Love Me* down to Walbaum's office that week. Dwarfed in a large leather chair, Walbaum sat with arms crossed behind his head, a touch of foam from his cappuccino on the tip of his nose. He listened to the song three times. He was volatile, a nervous little thing, and he loved *All the Crazies Love Me.* He called it a hit. Before their meeting was up, Walbaum was singing the chorus aloud, to Henry:

She must have read the sign,
On my head,
Which said,
Free love for the crazies.

That's good, Henry. That's quality.

I'm glad you enjoy it, Zachary.

I do. I do.

With Walbaum leading the way, *All the Crazies Love Me* was covered, and to Henry's liking, by Bobby Jacques, a French female vocal artist who went on to break the top twenty pop charts with the song in Europe and South America. On its success Henry had made good money—money which had all been spent. What remained was a feeling of great humiliation. Dr. Andrews refused to see him again. She never answered his calls. She cut him off. Henry thought his good health must have threatened her. She liked him weak, dizzy. Whatever the truth, the sting of shame often snuck up on him, in the shower, on the subway. Anywhere. Andrews. 9/11. Dizziness. The words were poison to Henry. Even here, though far from Andrews' apartment, her practice, he feared she might appear out of nowhere. New York was two-faced that way. Sometimes the Walbaums manifested. At other times it was old lovers who turned up. Never once had Henry and Andrews run into each other.

And thank god, said Henry, to himself.

But how had he ended up here? Just ahead was Alice Tully Hall, Juilliard. Paula lived two blocks further, off Columbus. He'd walked himself back to the West Side. It was the strangest thing—he'd never done anything like it. And how many cars had nearly run him over? An air conditioner could have fallen from a window missing him by feet and he didn't think he would have noticed. He stopped at the corner, awaiting a *walk* signal. Across the street a farmer's market lined the sidewalk. His eyes searched down the row of vendors for a flower stand. I'll buy some, he thought, to brighten up the home with. He cupped his hand above his brow to keep out glare. He saw one vendor was selling honey, another berries, another fresh cheeses. There were meat dealers offering bacon, pork chops and ground beef, and others selling pickled anything: onions, okra, cucumbers, peppers, tomatoes. He was about to give up—it seemed there were no flowers sold here—but his gaze fixed on Paula. She was there, browsing through a crate of apples. Saying her name aloud, happily, he grinned. She must have finished early with her parents and gone home. It felt like a great stroke of luck. He would like to go back to her place, lie down next to her, and sleep. What a morning it had been. He needed her touch, was desperate for it.

He saw the traffic light turn yellow, and prepared to cross. Yet when the signal changed, Henry stood still. The filter had risen behind his eyes. He felt like he might tip over or lose control of himself altogether. Dr. Jeffrey Moss, Paula's old lover, her violin teacher, her guide and mentor, had appeared beside her and was looking through the same crate of apples. Henry grabbed the gray pole of a traffic light, holding to it. He watched them with large, violent eyes. What was she doing with him? Had she not gone to meet her parents? Had she lied about that? But if this were true…

The strong impulse to come stomping at them now, like a lunatic, and begin screaming and throwing his fists, was storming through him. He knew that he'd regret that, perhaps forever, though. So he'd hold it together.

You must, he thought. You absolutely must.

But reining in his fury was difficult. While waiting for this to happen, he followed them up the sidewalk, towards Central Park.

Paula had changed clothes since this morning. But it wasn't uncommon for her to be as dolled up as she was now. Even if she were going from her apartment to the market and back home she did put on makeup and a flattering top and nice shoes, for you never knew just who you'd see out there in the streets of New York. Perhaps someone *big*. Of course, this short black skirt and tight fitting red top which cut low at the breasts, Henry understood perfectly. And it had nothing to do with a chance run-in with Itzhak Pearlman.

Sickening, said Henry, to himself. Just sickening.

Moss, himself, looked quite *debonair* in a tweed suit, his brown curls rising from his head like the snakes of the Gorgon. His gait, Henry noted, was asinine. He shifted left and right at the waist with every step, like a runway model. But why couldn't he walk like a normal person? Why did he have to call attention to himself at all times? Had no one loved him as a child? Had someone loved him *too* much?

They entered Central Park.

Henry, pulling nervously on the skin of his neck, strode behind rows of thick bushes and tall elms, keeping one eye on Moss and Paula and the other on the unsmooth soil below, careful not to trip on any fallen branches or divots in the ground. When Henry first met Paula, she and Moss had just ended a year-long affair. It was a joint-decision. They remained good friends. Henry was introduced to him at a cocktail party shortly after. Moss was not the good-looking man Paula had prepared him for. Under six feet tall, he was inches shorter than Henry. He had brown hair which rose up into high disorderly curls. His neck was short. Paula believed there were wise lines in his face, that his nose was formidable, that his eyes were dark and sensuous, *feeling*. As far as Henry could tell, none of this was true. The professor had been experimenting with facial hair, and Paula had been encouraging him, first with a pencil thin mustache, then a goatee, which lasted only three days, and finally a short beard. That night he was cleanly shaven. Paula thought the look suited him best. She volunteered the information to Henry. (And it fueled him in his pursuit.) She said Moss had taught her so much about herself, and that he had so much more to show her. Henry didn't see how this was possible. What could Moss teach Paula about herself?

For one thing, how to *be* myself, she had told him.

You couldn't convince Henry of this. Moss was too much of a phony to instruct Paula this way. Whatever the real answer, Moss had promised Paula big recitals after her graduation. He'd said he'd make sure she played for the most influential people in the field of classical music, who were all his good friends. He would get her career on the right path so that she could soar. On some days Henry felt certain that Moss was only there to help Paula. On others he imagined they were still sleeping with each other between classes. However, under no conditions would he play the jealous lover. He'd try and be cool. It was the only way. For in a woman jealousy was ugly, in a man it was downright pitiful, and made manifest it would send Paula straight out the door.

Just now, at a distance of some fifteen feet he followed mentor and disciple to the Bethesda Terrace, descending the grand limestone steps just moments after they had. Crowds of people were gathered here, the bronzed, winged angel rising up towards the wide-open sky. A saxophonist played *Putting On the Ritz.* Tourists posed for photos and the Rambles flowed green and urban-wild in the distance. Henry's heart thumped, watching Moss usher Paula up a crowded path towards the Boat House. But were they...Could they possibly be...Oh, lord. They were renting a boat. Paula had asked Henry to do it with her so many times, but he'd always said, Another day. Or, Who do you think is going to do all the rowing, *you?*

Observing them from behind a tree the strength of Henry's body intensified along with his anger. A boat was *too* romantic. He had to stop them. He took his phone from his pocket. His plan was simple, to call her and ask one question:

Are you with me or against me?

His throat was dry, tender. Seeing the time on his phone was two-thirty, he pressed *talk*. Pensive and dripping sweat, he awaited that pleasured twist of Paula's lips. She loved receiving calls. The thrill, it would never wear off. When it happened, her lips did their usual contortion, and she reached in her purse for her phone. She stared at it. Her expression changed from thoughtful to uncertain. The professor asked her a question. She shook her head, and put the phone back inside her purse. Henry watched, rancor filling his breast. He called again. This time she sent him to *voicemail.*

You bitch! he cried.

Moss and Paula set off in a boat. Henry, without the necessary cash to rent one of his own (the cost was $12-an-hour, plus a $20 deposit. He had $14 in his wallet, and credit cards weren't accepted), had to pursue them by land.

He took off after them.

From the cast-iron splendor of the Bow Bridge to the rocky shores of the Rambles, and further, Henry sprinted, hiked and stumbled. A dozen times he lost Moss and Paula, only to discover them rowing near an idyllic patch of reeds, enjoying the quiet calm of their surroundings. Moss had begun smoking a cigar. At times Paula smoked it, too. To Henry, watching from the shore, she appeared to take pleasure in turning it between her fingers. It made her look almost suave. But she wasn't a smoker. And Henry wanted to kill her. To kill them both.

The sun was beating down hot. Henry, with his hands on his knees, had a desperate thirst. He spotted a vendor under a canopy of twisting branches. He paid for a water, guzzling it down. Trotting along the pond's edge, he wondered if he didn't have all this coming to him. After all, Paula was Moss' before she was Henry's. He couldn't destroy their bond, nor could he do anything for her, professionally. His contribution was strictly romantic. But more than romance, Paula wanted success. A breeze was crossing over the water and Henry, feeling its coolness against his damp skin, looked out at the pond. Their boat was stopped, and Henry kneeled in the dirt, resting. The sun was so bright on the boat slowly drifting some thirty feet in the distance that their bodies were all but whitened out. Trying not to lose them, Henry, lifting his head, stood so close to the water, he nearly fell in. He held onto a tree branch overhead. The sun was too much. He couldn't see them. But what *couldn't* he see? Were they holding each other? Was Moss caressing her face? Was he kissing her? But *was* he?

Henry, shaking hot and cold at the same time, turned in disgust. His vision darkened, and he braced himself against a garbage can. What had they been doing? He was positive he knew. His whole body suffered the information. His toes hurt, his ears, too. He told himself he had to move, to get out of here. He walked rapidly towards the exit of the park, hitting the low hung branches of the trees with an open hand. He kicked at the dirt and threw his fist in the air. On Fifth

Avenue, anger no longer stunted the flow of his thoughts. Had he ever loved her? No. He hadn't. So why had he stayed with her so long? Because he'd been under a spell. That was it. What joy had he ever received? Every moment riddled with difficulties. And for *what?* His skin felt like it was burning. The noise of cars and construction further disturbed his balance. He hurried down shadowed side-streets, his arms swinging fiercely. He tried to determine at what he could direct the violent feeling in his heart. He felt at any moment he might smash the windshield of a parked car or pull the long dark vines from the side of a townhouse. He had to exert force onto something. In a bus shelter, he raised his cell phone over his head, then pulled up the moment before releasing it.

He was glad he hadn't destroyed his phone, an hour later Paula called. He was home. Though beside himself with anger, his tone was even-keeled. He asked about her family. How were they doing?

They're fine, Paula answered him. We had breakfast, but they had theater tickets so I met Jeffrey for lunch.

Henry was pouring himself a drink in the kitchen, shaking. He said, Where did you go, the two of you?

To the Boathouse, she answered. We got in one of those silly boats. It was Jeffrey's idea.

Paula always told him what she and Moss did together. She felt no need to lie, nor anything to hide. After all, he was her *mentor.*

Did you have a good time? said Henry, darkly.

Fine, she told him. How are you doing? How's your back?

He didn't understand the question. His back? Walking from the kitchen to the bedroom, climbing into bed with his drink, spilling vodka on the sheets, he remembered, however.

Right, *my back*, he said.

He told her she had no reason to worry, he was fine. A minor procedure would likely be necessary, that was all. First he'd need to have an MRI, which would happen early in the morning, before the graduation.

I won't be late, though.

Take your time, she said to him.

It'll be fast, he assured her. I'll make it by ten.

Okay, Henry.

Earlier she'd invited him to dinner with her parents for this evening, seven-thirty. Henry had declined. She asked again now if he'd like to come.

I'm going to stay home and take it easy, he said.

Are you sure? We're going to the Oyster Bar. It's so close to you.

He considered for a moment. If he didn't attend the dinner, would Moss go in his place? Paula's parents were very fond of him. They liked to see the doctor of the violin when they were in town. Henry would never tell Marcel and Denise Mills that the forty-seven year old had dated their daughter for a whole year. It was, for Paula, a secret to be kept from them. She wouldn't forgive Henry if he ever disclosed this information. But dinner was out of the question. He was too exhausted.

I can't.

All right, she said. I'll see you in the morning.

Hanging up his phone, he drew the bedcovers to his chin. Though late afternoon, he didn't doubt, with the blinds closed, that he'd be able to sleep till morning. He wouldn't have to read to tire out his eyes, the lids were already so heavy. Drifting off, he began to compose a song in his head. If he were going to remember it the next day, he should write it down, he thought. On the nightstand, cluttered with magazines and empty water glasses, used tissues, was a pad kept exactly for this purpose. However, Henry didn't have the will to sit up and write. Maybe it'll come back to you in the morning, he said, to himself. The words'll be right there, in your head.

Deciding this was true, and closing in on sleep, he sang the lyrics again to himself:

You didn't tell her about your cancer.
Her story interfered, and you didn't have the chance.
But it'll be just that much more simple to say it,
In person.
Tomorrow.
Tomorrow, you'll tell her everything. Tomorrow.

TWO

Dahl said he'd had to pull strings to get Henry squeezed in for an ultrasound at nine the following morning. But, nine was still cutting it close. The graduation started at ten, and Henry wanted to be on time. He let the person in charge know as much as soon as he arrived for his appointment. The technologist was unsympathetic. She wouldn't be hurried. Henry, disguising his irritation with a grateful, pliant tone, said he understood her position, she had a job to do, and she didn't want to be told how to do it. Yet his girlfriend's graduation began in less than an hour and he still had to get to the West Side. So if she could just pick up the pace a little, that would be terrific.

Thank you. I appreciate it. You understand, he said, to the technologist.

She told Henry to be quiet. It's *you* who's adding time to the procedure.

She was a short, stout redhead. Her eyes were a dark blue, full of malice. Pointing the transducer, like a pistol, at his crotch, she asked him to hold his breath and be still.

Okay, said Henry. I'm sorry.

It was the third stop on the doctor-go-round, this, a small room set in low light in Cornell Hospital on York Avenue. Henry sat motionlessly on a halfway elevated table. Minutes prior, after changing into a gown and sitting, his testicles had been propped on a towel by the technologist and lathered with gel, causing his scrotum to tighten up against the cold air blowing from the vents. Over his scrotum, the transducer was being drawn, east, west, north and south. The technologist reminded him again to be still. After several more minutes of the same, she placed the transducer down and said she'd return—without specifying when—and left the room.

Naked below the waist, Henry's thoughts shifted to the subject of prosthetic testicles. Before leaving Dahl's office yesterday the doctor had told him about this option. By and large he'd said men were pleased with their prosthetics. Henry had asked if his scrotum would be more *flappy* if he went without one and the doctor had told him that it would be precisely that. Furthermore, as far as his sexual opportunities went—and the term seemed an invention of the doctor's—he might do better all around. A woman would hardly know the difference. They were slightly firmer, the prosthetics, but shaped almost like the real thing.

Henry hadn't given it any more thought since yesterday. Yet he realized, with the technologist returning to the room, not alone, but with her superior, who introduced himself to Henry as Dr. Munson, and said he would be doing a second ultrasound, that a prosthetic was something to take seriously.

This second ultrasound was an inauspicious sign. Dr. Munson, who had a salt and pepper mustache and a nose which was shaped like a walnut, gave Henry's scrotum an additional once over with the transducer. Then he placed the instrument down and said, to him:

Mr. Schiller, I'm sorry. You have cancer of the testicles. Almost definitely, sir.

Henry nodded his head.

I'm *so* sorry.

Thank you, said Henry.

Are you all right? I'm here to talk.

But there was no time for discussion. The graduation started in four minutes and he wouldn't let the doctor waste another minute of his time. Henry dressed and hurried out the door. He called Paula from a taxi. She was seated in the full auditorium. Where was *he*?

I'm entering the building, he lied.

Oh, good. What happened with the MRI?

Behind her he could hear the sound of a thousand voices. He said, I'm going to be all right.

What did they say it was?

Henry, glancing at the dirty floor of the taxi, said, I have a *bulge*.

A bulge?

Yes. A bulge in my back.

I've never heard of that.

Neither had I.

So it's rare?

Sort of, he said.

How do they treat it?

Henry, pressing on closed eyelids with thumb and forefinger, said, Really, I have to get more details from the doctor.

But you're going to be okay?

I'll be fine. There's nothing to worry about.

That's a relief, she said. I'll see you after the graduation.

Correct.

He hung up. Compared to the strong rain of past days, Henry had figured there'd be less traffic and he would make good time to the West Side. But cars were backed up through Central Park. He was inching his way through the transverse, his nerves roiled. And yet he'd tell Paula the truth. However, today was her graduation.

So let her enjoy it. Give her this moment.

Don't make it,
About you,
And your,
Test,
Icles.

Nearly through the park, he passed fifteen dollars through the slot, got out of the car and ran. Pumping his arms and legs unsettled his groin. But what difference did it make? He had to get to Alice Tully Hall, now. He emerged onto Central Park West, down 67th Street to Broadway, and was inside the auditorium five minutes later, glad to see others passing through the doors with him. Up on stage was a woman talking about *the great moments in a young person's life*, adding, ironically, that this was not one of them.

Because you want to be out there—her fist shot into the air—taking on life. Don't worry, your time is coming.

The house lights were turned down, and bright beams shone from above the stage. The first rows of seats were reserved for graduates. At the back of the auditorium, Henry anxiously looked for Paula. There were so many students in white cap and gown, he couldn't distinguish her from the others. He located her parents near the center aisle. Her father, Marcel, broad-shouldered, amiable, smart, and with his bald head shaved clean for the occasion. And beside him, Paula's stepmother, Denise, sitting up straight, her head of short blond hair newly dyed and cut. He didn't look forward to the lunch. Not that he minded these two. But would he have the energy? His whole body wanted to collapse. He looked down the back aisle for a seat. Each one was occupied. He could do no better than lean on a column.

Applause followed the speaker offstage, and a young woman stepped out into the spotlight. Henry had met many of Paula's classmates. It wasn't a very large school. But who was this? A knockout. And that red dress, so confident and sexy, bought new for the occasion, thought Henry. This young woman was collecting her strength, gathering it all at the diaphragm. Her face, full of rich emotion, turned towards the floor. She took another deep breath. (Henry took one with her.) Lifting her head with new purpose in its every rising inch she began to sing. Her arms circled dramatically in the air. A sound was projecting from her being, a truthful, potent sonic explosion. The full audience was in her thrall. Henry glanced, at one face and another, and at a half-dozen more, confirming as much to himself. This attractive flower, built not so big, nor small, but with long black hair, and a spectacularly red mouth which released a single, booming note—she was a miracle of feminine beauty, and vocal skill.

She is a siren, said Henry, in a whisper.

Oh, she is something,
I could be,
The man I want,
To be,
With a woman,
Like her.

When she was finished, Henry began to clap, slowly at first, then wildly. The singer, swinging forward with her arms, bowed, so that the tips of her fingers nearly brushed the floor. Awestruck, Henry screamed:

Bravo! Bravo! Encore!

This feeling of uplift, could it stay with him? He'd need it after the ceremony, with all the socializing he had before him. The excitement produced by that woman's singing would carry him through it. During the next hour Henry stood, clinging to an idea of the singer. Following the ceremony, leaving Alice Tully Hall, Jeffrey Moss walked only several feet ahead of him. Henry ducked away, not wanting to speak to him. Thank god the graduation would mark the start of less Moss in Paula's life. After all, she would no longer be enrolled in his class. The spontaneous after-school drink with that doctor of the violin could no longer be spontaneous, but would require arranging. And Paula was so busy. Her practice schedule was rigorous. She wouldn't have the time to see him. Henry wouldn't have to hear his name mentioned daily. He'd looked forward to this for a long time.

Out on Broadway, he located Paula. She was surrounded by a crowd of well-wishers. He couldn't get near to her. He greeted her stepmother, instead, kissing her cheek, shook Marcel's hand, congratulating them both. The sun beat hard against his back. His navy suit was made of linen, yet still he was so warm. Where was that singer? The sidewalk was thronged. Making out any one person was difficult. He wanted a last look at her, though, to clear away the sinking feeling in his heart.

A hand fell strong against his back. It was Denise Mills.

Henry, she said, I don't think you've ever been introduced to Carla Frank, *Gina* Frank's mother.

How are you? he said, shaking with Ms. Frank.

She was an unhealthily thin woman, of below average height. Crooked vertical lines ran alongside her mouth. Her blue eyes looked confusedly at Denise. She said, This is the one who writes the songs?

This is my *daughter's* boyfriend. She only *has* one. And he wrote a hit song, Denise insisted.

A miserable grin commanded Henry's face. It was how she introduced him to any stranger. It must stop. *All the Crazies Love Me* was old news.

Henry's songs are very good, Carla.

Are you having any luck these days? Ms. Frank asked him.

No. Not really, he said. He looked once around for Paula. It seemed she was gone.

I hear that's a hard racket, said Ms. Frank.

As hard as any, Henry answered her. With his hands in his pockets, his gaze would neither stay in one place, nor focus on anyone or anything.

You've got to love what you do, Ms. Frank told him. That's the important thing.

That's what they say.

Henry's just being modest, said Denise. Like always, she was rocking back on her heels. All that buoyancy explained how she stayed so thin. She said, Henry almost sold a jingle.

Really? went Ms. Frank.

A Swedish clothing company, Denise continued, was after a song for a new promotional campaign. They were going to go with Henry's, but changed their minds at the last minute.

That's too bad, offered Ms. Frank. Next time.

Henry didn't know why Paula even told her stepmother these things, it was humiliating, insulting. Struggling to remain polite, he said, I never meant to get involved in jingle-writing in the first place. I don't mean to put more crap into the world.

Suddenly Henry winced, clutching his chest.

Are you okay? Denise asked.

Do you need a pain-killer? I have pain-killers. Ms. Frank reached into her leather purse, but came up empty and apologized.

I'm all right, said Henry. I'm fine.

But this wasn't the place for him to stand and he excused himself, saying he'd go check-in on Paula.

At once, he was caught in a swarm of people. Fighting to get free, he slid between graduates into an open space, near the curb. It was here that he found himself behind the graduation singer. Taking in this face up close he lowered his eyes. Was it her? Yes. Yes, it was. He stole another glance, and this time she caught him and he quickly looked back at the sidewalk. And why did he do that—he didn't know. But the sun was high above them. Along the pavement Henry saw her shadow made out an excitingly curvy figure with hair, by the same adumbrated token, full and luxurious.

Oh god, he said to himself, this is some gal.

So many shrill voices engulfed him. A tension was pulling in the air between she and Henry. He could feel it in his neck and his piano-strong hands. He wanted to know everything about her. And if he had her to himself, what would he ask? What did he want to know most of all? The question excited him. She was now joined by a friend who addressed her by her name, which was Moira. A lovely name, it warmed Henry to hear Moira speak, her voice, kind and honest, full of depth. She was discussing plans for the coming evening. She said she wanted to have a good time, that she was ready for anything. Tonight was the night of her college graduation and she wouldn't let it go to waste.

We're going to start the night at Clover's, on Sullivan, said her friend.

Henry blushed, and his chest rose. Clover's. On Sullivan. He'd never heard of it. Perhaps he'd end up there himself. He laughed at the thought. To himself, he sang:

Early evening, and I leave Paula,
In the name of poor health.
Home for a primping, then I,
Taxi down to Clover's,
Arriving at 9.
Staking out a place at the bar,
And from there I wait,
Until Moira enters.
And because her friends are yet to show,
She comes to stand alone at the bar.
There are no stools, so I offer mine.
And when she refuses to accept it,
I say to her, Wait. Wait, but I know you.
I do.
Didn't you perform today at the,
Juilliard graduation?
It's you.
You were phenomenal. A triumph.
The best I've ever seen.
At which point…

His singing abruptly ended. Something frantic stretched through his breast. His cheeks were burning hot. He rose up onto his tiptoes, staring in the distance. His vision fogged, he couldn't make out what his eyes had seen only a moment before. Edging forward, his head felt heavy. But who was it out there? Paula? And beside her, Jeffrey Moss?

On the street named for Bernstein, amid hundreds of revelers, Henry fought through the crowd. From inside his head arose an imbalanced feeling, his chest burst heat. He drew around a graduate, his fingers slipping from her white gown. He strode past a group photo. Soreness came into his testicle. He put his hand to his pants, holding them to his body. One thought dominated his mind: he must get between Paula and Moss. And when he was within five feet of them, he stopped short. What had made his legs feel so weighted-down? He listened to teacher and student speak to one another. There was too much celebration happening on all sides of him to hear precisely what they said. But the tone, thought Henry, *the tone* was the same used by lovers.

Hello Doctor Moss, said Henry, putting out his hand to shake.

Moss took Henry's hand, gripping it firmly. The coils of brown hair were springing wildly from his head this morning. A mustache was there above his upper lip.

Henry, he said, I'd been onto something before you showed. Yes, I'd been asking Paula if the little dogs were going to pieces. And so dear…are they?

Paula covered her mouth, subduing a strange laughter.

Are they dressing at least?

Jeffrey, *stop*, Paula implored him.

Through hot eyes Henry smiled at a joke which he didn't understand. He took a protective, albeit small, step closer to Paula. Moss, himself, was standing on top of her.

Could she smell his aftershave? It was splintering Henry's nostrils. At the back of his throat was its strong menthol odor. Moss was positioned on what Paula called her *good right side.* In contrast to the left, the eye was perfectly almond shaped, the teeth straight, not jagged, her skin generally clearer.

I was in Paris last week, said the doctor of the violin, his eyes focusing intently on Paula, and do you know who I saw while there? Monsieur Michel Drouot. And I told him he'd be very fortunate if I let him hear you play.

Did you?

I did, Paula.

The name Michel Drouot meant nothing to Henry. Or perhaps it did, because at once he set a hand on Paula's hip and his head began to hover possessively above her bare shoulder.

You should have seen Drouot's face when I told Boris Lang the same. We were having drinks near the Opera House. Michel got so angry. He said, You told me that I'd have the first exclusive recital at my home with Paula Mills. What are you trying to do?

So you're saying he was mad?

Oui, Madame. And that's how we want him.

Paula took Henry's hand from her hip, kissed it, and returned it to the air. Even as Henry felt mildly spurned—she'd given his hand a kind of harsh toss-off—he still shot Moss a look, one that said, Well there you have it, she's mine and I'm hers, so get lost.

But Moss, with his head tilted back, didn't acknowledge it. His eyes were closed, and he was saying:

Gertrude Hausmann pulled me aside after we'd left the café. What a woman, cunning, deadly. She asked me, When do I get to meet Ms. Mills? I said, Be patient. Your time will come. She's in New York, sitting in on a record with Yo-Yo Ma. How's that for savvy?

Very savvy, she assured him.

Henry's thighs were profusely sweating. He didn't want to be here. They should go to lunch. It was time. Henry signaled to Paula's father.

Our reservation's in twenty minutes. We should really get going.

Marcel, in agreement, took his wife by the arm and they began saying their goodbyes to Jeffrey Moss. The way the professor looked at Paula, it was all so clear: he was fucking her. Henry couldn't blame Marcel and Denise for not seeing it. A parent's vision was strictly impaired in such cases, taking in solely the purest meaning of everything. What with Paula's stepmother holding Moss so tightly in her arms, and her father calling him a great man. Meanwhile a polite smile persisted on Henry's face, and in his heart was the firm desire to break the professor's teeth.

Finally Henry was alone with the Mills. They rode in a taxi to the Four Seasons, Marcel sitting up front with the driver. Henry was on the back seat pressed between Paula and Denise. All the Mills' in look and spirit were positively blooming.

Accepting your diploma, you were just beautiful, Denise said. And *so* mature.

Marcel reached back through the partition to take Paula's hand.

My girl, he said, with these fingers, so special. We love you so much.

And I love *you* both so much.

Henry watched their family's heart collectively lift. But in his head, he was singing:

A thousand curious aches,
In the course of a lifetime.
Why get unsettled,
Mentally?
For the belly rails,
The brain ails,
The heart, it wails.
And you keep going.

Isn't that just utter crap, he said, to himself.

Out of the taxi and walking towards Lexington on 52nd and Park, through a fog of thin gray smoke billowing from a kebab stand with its sizzling lamb and chicken skewers, Henry was in a daze. In the bones of his fingers was some unknown pain. Could it be related to his cancer? How so? he asked himself, undoing the top button of his shirt. He needed air, his chest was tight. Lifting his arms, he tried to loosen the muscles there. He wouldn't pass out. And if he did, he had Paula's father right beside him. He would help me, thought Henry, assuming he noticed the fall. Marcel was so absorbed in the moment of his daughter's big day. A bulky man, his check suit was short at the sleeves, tight in the shoulders. It didn't affect his manner in the least. He seemed full of reward for his fatherly service. He'd done everything for Paula: the summers of violin instruction, all those tickets to the Philharmonic, and his love. He loved her so much, and she loved him, too.

Sweetheart, come, Marcel said to his daughter.

Paula went to him. Cradling her in his arms, Marcel smiled. He said, Paula, you're all grown, and the world is at your fingertips. You've done everything you've set out to do. The truth is, we're in awe of you.

Denise said, Go on, Marcel, give it to her.

Paula's father reached inside the breast pocket of his jacket. A cloud passed in front of the sun, playing its games of shadow and light. Marcel, large and pulsating with excitement, placed an envelope in his daughter's palm. For all your hard work, he said.

Paula, to no one in particular, went, *A gift?* then began carefully peeling back the seal of the envelope. She looked up at her parents, smiling. She was so delicate with the envelope.

Marcel finally shouted, Come on, baby, just tear it open.

Paula laughed at herself, then ripped through the dented white envelope. Her fingers began walking through the important papers inside. Suddenly, her head shot up, and she cried out:

Oh...my...god.

Walking in through the Four Seasons, where important people lunched—those persons who made the city rich or poor or rich again—Henry's face felt cold, his stomach sick. Following the maître d' towards the dining room with its famous pools his mind struggled for calm. The Mills had given their greatest achievement a check for $25,000 and told her she should travel throughout Europe this summer. They said it was important that she take the time, for once her professional life started up it would be very difficult for her to get away from her responsibilities and nearly impossible to do so without the feeling that something was pulling her back. Paula, wrapping smooth pink arms of appreciation, first around her father's neck, then her stepmother's, had given Henry a look which asked him to share in the euphoria of the moment. He'd tried, but couldn't. In the full dining room with the currents of power flowing all around him, he was silent. His mind was unthinking, a blank. Under the table, Paula took Henry's hand, squeezing it, and said, Maybe we'll meet in Europe.

Maybe, he said.

They were the only words he uttered during the meal. He hardly touched his lobster. Paula, surrounded by Henry, her father and stepmother, on the day of her graduation, with twenty-five grand in her pocket, was bursting with confidence.

Raising her glass in the air, she said, To learning nothing at college. *Here here.*

To learning *nothing?* said Denise, aghast.

I was born for the real world, Paula told her. At ten I should have jumped in. Dad, why didn't you push me?

Push you out of the house? Never, he replied with a shake of the head.

Paula said, I'd have been ready, and she took a bottle of champagne from an ice bucket. A waiter rushed to assist her, but she waved him off. Setting a full glass on the table, her blue eyes emitted glee. She wore a strapless black dress that stopped at the thighs. Her solid legs were crossed. She sat up tall, her grin full of self-belief. Addressing her father, she said, I could have used my time better, that's all I'm saying. Life is short.

Marcel, his robust shoulders becoming even fuller now, said, You're a very smart woman. You'll understand why I did what I did one day.

Did you fear the professional world would have made me unrecognizable to you? It could still happen.

Marcel flashed her a look of horror. Paula saw this. She kissed his cheek.

I'm just saying I've got a lot to do.

And you'll do it all.

Henry was perfectly still in his chair. Only his eyes moved, back and forth, from one speaker to the next. But even this was exhausting.

What I want is hard to get, said Paula. Her arms were crossed, her chin up high. Some atrociousness will be necessary.

Like what? demanded Denise.

Yes, like *what?* said her father.

Henry took his glass of champagne and shot it back. His throat burned from the carbonation, tears filling his eyes.

I'll have to be even more hard on myself.

Your mother taught you discipline. Every morning she woke you at four a.m. to do your scales.

Daddy, I'm grateful she did. I wouldn't be here if she had let me sleep.

She's missed so much in these last thirteen years. But she saw you at Carnegie Hall.

You'll always bring that up, said Paula to her father, adoringly.

Marcel smiled, the memory coming back to him. Paula was in the *Five Under Ten Masters-to-Be* concert series. She played Schubert. She brought down the house. Your mother was so proud of you that day.

She made me go home and practice after the show, said Paula, unemotionally. Mistakes had been made during the performance.

She was hard on you, her father admitted.

I could take it, said Paula, clicking her tongue.

She removed you from school for two years shortly after.

And my playing shot up.

Her father agreed, with a solid nod of his head. But for you those were hard times.

That's not how I remember them.

A lot of tears.

We all need a motivator. I had the best.

You did, Paula.

She told me I would be one of the great violinists of my time.

She told you that, seconded Marcel.

I'm sorry she's not here today.

But she saw you at Carnegie Hall.

You're right, Daddy, she did.

When lunch concluded they strolled uptown along sunny Madison, window-shopping. Henry was impatient to go home. Still, he gawked with Paula, her father and stepmother, at dresses and diamond jewelry in windows. Then his phone began to ring. It was Dahl. Henry went cold. Without saying anything, he fell back behind the Mills' and answered. Dahl asked him if it were a good time to talk. Henry said it was as good a time as any. To which Dahl assured him that these first days would be especially hard, he should go easy on himself.

We have some important things to discuss. So, if you'd just give me your attention for a moment. I want to schedule the orchiectomy for this Monday. What do you say?

This Monday? said Henry. That's three days from now.

If we could do it today, we would.

This is all coming so fast.

I understand.

You're sure it has to be Monday?

I'm sure, Henry.

Then I'll do it Monday, he said, in a whisper.

What did you decide about the prosthetic?

I'm going to take one.

Dahl said, I think that's the right decision.

The doctor started to explain the operation. He told Henry he'd be put to sleep with an anesthetic. They'd go through the lining of the stomach into the scrotum and remove the testicle. At most only one night would be spent in the hospital, but in all likelihood he could leave the same day.

Will there be someone to take you home from the hospital?

My girlfriend, Paula.

Dahl told him it was hospital policy that he be released into someone's care, but also there'd be some physical discomfort and he'd need help getting around at first. In the case of a surgery like this, some responded better than others. The doctor at the hospital would suggest Henry have his CT-scans administered when he awoke from the operation, and if he were feeling well enough, he should do it then so they could have all of the critical information about the spread of the cancer as soon as possible. In addition to this, however, there was the matter of his sperm.

Henry's lips turned out and his bloodshot eyes averted to the sky.

We'll need to have a sample put away tomorrow.

Tomorrow?

Henry, you never know what'll happen during an operation like this. So, we need to get some sperm in a bank.

And that happens *tomorrow?*

Or, if you like, you can overnight your semen to their offices.

Overnight it? *Really?*

So you'll do it at the bank?

I guess I will.

By the time Henry was off with Dahl, the party had arrived outside the Carlyle Hotel. The Mills' suggested a round of drinks at Bemelman's. Henry agreed. But as soon as he walked in the door he regretted it, for there was Andy Powell seated at the piano at the center of the room, dressed in a black tuxedo, playing *After You've Gone.* He had a vibrant look, a real glow. Henry knew him from around the clubs. But he couldn't stand Powell, or his playing. He thought it lacked feel, heart, love, knowledge, instinct. He struck notes which didn't balance order with disorder or reconcile past with present and future. His meanings, they were too straight, missed the curves, the bumps, hadn't the sense of failure about them or the propinquity to the abyss, the void, which was necessary for not only true greatness, but even moderate goodness. And he looks like an asshole, too. That grin, shit-eating. Henry would like to wipe it off his face. So the Carlyle gig was better than Henry's at the Beekman. *So* what. Henry didn't care. *He* was a songwriter. That's what *he* did. The Beekman was a way of earning money, he wouldn't do it forever. As it were, though, he should call his boss, Edgar Diaz and tell him he'd have to take some time off from work.

They sat down in a booth. A round of martinis were ordered. The darkened room was almost at capacity, the lights, soft bursts of gold along the walls. Paula and Marcel sunk into private conversation. Powell was onto *Ain't Misbehavin'.* Denise, swaying side to side, told Henry she loved this song, it reminded her of dancing with her father as a child. Henry, who played it most nights at the Beekman—and did a much better rendition than Powell ever could—said, Well that's great, Denise. Please, excuse me a moment.

Henry went to stand out on Madison. The sun was still strong in the sky. He stared long at his phone. That he felt anxious about making this call struck him as odd. What was the feeling about, anyway? He hadn't done anything wrong. He was sick. Perhaps dying. Anyway, he and Edgar Diaz got on well together. (If he wasn't his boss, he might even call him a friend.) It was one and a half years ago that Henry had tried out for the job and Edgar had hired Henry on the spot. He'd even called him *the one*. (Nobody had ever called Henry that.) For eighteen months Henry had showed up on time. Never once had he called out sick. There'd been the incident with John Grover, but Edgar couldn't still hold that against him, could he? Besides Grover was a nasty old drunk, and *he'd* been the one to accost Henry and not the other way around.

It had been his second month on the job. Grover, a *rapporteur* for the U.N. on sex crimes against children in sub-Saharan Africa, had come in from a full day of addressing the General Assembly. That frail but hostile curmudgeon Grover with his blue metallic eyes and the long white hairs growing out his nose and his habit of throwing around his weight and telling you what to do and then criticizing you for it afterwards:

Kid, play some Tatum. *Ahhh*, you'll stink it up. You can't do speed *and* style. So do some Fats. No, never mind. You're no good.

Edgar had warned Henry about Grover. Ignore his bad manners, he'd said.

Grover was a troubled man, broken by visions of deprivation and bloodshed and mass graves during five decades of service in Africa. He could not take this world of New York City and the Beekman Hotel seriously, said Edgar. But nevertheless he came in to get drunk, and when he drank he was hostile, at times plain violent.

Just let him be. You think you can do that? Edgar had asked him.

Won't be a problem, sir.

Don't engage.

I won't.

Perhaps Grover had put back six or seven old-fashioneds that fateful evening. It was late, almost eleven-thirty. Grover, seated in the lounge over four hours, from nowhere approached the piano. Henry didn't see him coming, his attention was on playing. He'd never have anticipated Grover dumping a mixture of bourbon and muddled fruit into his lap. But he did. Henry jumped to his feet. He was horrified, incensed. Somehow he recalled Edgar's instructions and quickly gathered his emotions, sweeping them back into his heart, and did nothing but ask Grover to leave.

Leave? *You* leave, the old man had shouted.

I work here.

Ahh, screw *you.* Grover stood with his forefinger aimed at Henry. In a gray double-breasted suit, he was so frail. He told Henry he wasn't a man, that he knew it just by looking at him. I could eat you alive.

Henry had no idea what Grover had against him. He gave other employees at the Beekman a hard time, but with him he was especially cruel.

Just go home, said Henry.

In response, Grover shouted, Let's go. Outside. Me and you.

He'd been looking for a fight, to roll up his sleeves and go toe to toe with the piano player. Henry could kill him with a single punch. And he was *not* going to hurt an old man. Even after Grover came at his throat all Henry did was to hold him back. Grover would not acquiesce, he was vicious. At some point in restraining him, however, Henry used too much force and accidentally pushed Grover to the floor. Crowds gathered around them. Edgar wasn't happy that Grover, having thrown out his back, had to be wheeled from the lounge on a gurney. There'd been a small piece about it in the *Post* the next morning. The headline read:

Beekman Piano Player
K.O.'s Member of U.N.

Henry was sure he'd get fired. There'd been witnesses to the scene, though, those who saw Grover go after him. So they cut him a break. All the same, Henry knew the hotel management had their eye on him. Even one year later the incident had left Henry second-guessing his job security.

But that's just in your head, Henry told himself. Dial Edgar. Do it.

On his phone he pressed *talk*. In three rings Edgar answered. The sound of him pulling on a cigarette was a soft pop in Henry's ear. He said, What's happening, Hank? You've got problems?

Edgar was the only person who called Henry *Hank*. Henry didn't mind. In fact, he enjoyed it. It partly soothed the strained feeling in his chest now. He said, I'm sick, Edgar. I've got something bad.

What is it? Edgar's tone was severe. He was concerned.

Henry thought he'd tell him the truth. However, he became anxious and said, It's mono, Edgar.

Mono? Hmm, that can be tough, Hank. You must be laid up in bed?

I am.

You sound like you're on the street.

Actually, I'm heading back from the doctor's, said Henry, his voice unsteady. I've been in bed for days.

Sorry to hear that. I take it you'll be out a couple weeks. You'll want to get a lot of rest. Don't push yourself.

That's what the doctor told me.

He's right, Hank.

Edgar began speaking of his own experience with mononucleosis. His case had lasted over four months. Unable to work, he'd run into financial trouble. His wife had had to take a second job. He could hardly remember seeing her during that time. Edgar talked about the fatigue, the problems eating, but Henry wasn't listening. A man on the opposite side of the street, tall, about sixty-years-of-age, with short gray hair, had caught his attention. In blue jeans and a navy dress jacket the stranger's attire seemed distinctly of the West Coast. His gait was all sun and palm trees, ocean air. The man proceeded up 76th Street towards Fifth Avenue, Central Park.

Henry, his heart rate increased, said, I'm sorry, Edgar. I'll call you back.

He hung up. Crossing the street, the light already changing, Henry ran fast, sliding in his dress shoes. A taxi screamed towards him, but he gained the curb with an inch to spare. Past a roasted nut dealer he hurried. Was it really his father just up ahead? Art Schiller? Would Art come to New York and not tell him? Rushing up the sidewalk, his testicle was in pain. But what did that matter? Ten feet ahead of him was a man, his father. It did look like him. And Henry would never forgive him for this.

Sonovabitch. How could he. To come to New York and not tell me.

Moving fast beside a row of palatial limestone townhouses, and closing in on the man, Henry's nerves were an accident waiting to happen. His scalp prickled hot. Fifteen feet from his target, he cried, Hey, *you!*

The man didn't stop but turned into a building. Henry advanced quickly and was facing in at the doors a moment later, looking in through an austere marble lobby. The man was gone. Blood rose into Henry's cheeks. Holding his head, he asked the doorman if he could tell him the name of the person who'd just passed through the lobby. The doorman, a wide, beaver-ish-looking fellow, said he couldn't give out that information. Henry, his head hanging, retreated back to the hotel.

He called Edgar.

You sound all of out breath, Hank. You all right?

I'm fine.

What's the matter?

It's nothing. Nothing at all. I'm hoping to be back at work soon.

You'll see how you're feeling.

Maybe a week. Ten days, said Henry, still not listening to Edgar.

Just tell me if you need anything. Your job will be waiting for you.

Thank you, Edgar.

Off the phone and standing under the awning of the Carlyle, through his whole face, his forehead and cheeks, around the mouth and chin, were the creased lines of inner-turmoil. With his hand set on the back of his head, he began to feel great disappointment. To himself, he was saying, Probably wasn't really Dad. If only it had been. I'd have fallen on his shoulder and sobbed. Could use him more than ever.

It was as far he'd let his own heart swell. At once he corrected his overly curved posture, lifted his head, his neck and spine.

I become tired of myself when I think like this. You'll be fine. Just pull it together.

Adjusting from the sun on Madison to the low light of Bemelman's caused his eyes to make out dark amorphous spots which floated to the ceiling then disappeared. Paula welcomed Henry back. The martini had taken hold of her and she was sitting slumped-drunk in her chair. Marcel, big and cheerful, his shiny bald head teeming sweat, cried out for Henry to sit beside him, asking his wife to make room in the booth. Denise staggered into an adjacent chair.

Powell was onto *I've Got Rhythm*. Henry couldn't bear to listen. Christ, he could play it ten times better. He tried tuning out the instrument.

Marcel said, So Henry, how are you?

I'm great. Thank you. Really very well.

Paula's father was a chemist. Usually his time with Henry was spent encouraging him to think beyond his small world, to make sure not a single day passed without his considering the lifespan of a star, for instance, or the earth's boiling inner-core. It was tiresome. During their last dinner roughly three month ago, the extinction of bees had formed the basis of Marcel's speech. Dead bees, dead plants, dead people, he kept saying this over and over again. He'd spoken for an hour about the need for humans to regard bees with the same deference that they would their own gods, because without them there was no life, no us, no single human consciousness. Henry had left the dinner table that night with a crippling headache. The next day he'd written a song called, *Dead Bees. Dead Plants. Dead people.* Those were its only lyrics. It was another throw-away. Nothing for Zachary Walbaum.

However now, and for the first time, Marcel wanted to discuss Henry's songwriting. He even admitted to a kind of shame. His face a drunken red, he said he always talked about his own ideas with Henry.

Dating my daughter so long without my knowing what you really do, it's not right, is it? Tell me, Henry.

Tell you *what?*

Tell me how you write a song? How do you begin?

How do I *begin?*

Please, tell me what that entails?

Henry's cheeks went slack. He didn't want to talk about this. It wasn't the time. He said, Marcel, you just do it. The more thinking, the more discussion, the worse off you are.

A look of confusion formed on Marcel's face, and he said, So, you just begin? That's it? How do you know if something's done if you don't know where it's supposed to go in the first place?

Henry told him, It's just a feeling, Marcel. That's all.

Just a feeling?

Correct.

I see. I see. His brow furrowed. Paula told me you almost sold a jingle to a Swedish clothing company.

Well, *ye-es*, he said. But really that was nothing.

Not nothing, insisted Marcel. I would love to hear what this jingle sounds like. Perhaps you'd sing it for me.

Sing it?

Sure. Is that uncomfortable for you? Because if you'd just sing a part of it...that would be...just grand, Henry, grand.

Powell had gone on break. Henry's voice wouldn't have to compete with the piano. But this was ludicrous. He wasn't going to sing this *dead* jingle for Marcel. And to do it a cappella. *No.* Marcel was practically begging him, though. He said how much it upset him that he'd never heard Henry sing, not once.

I should be more supportive of you. I'm sorry I haven't been.

Henry, breaking up inside, looked at his martini. Taking a long sip, he said, Fine. You want to hear *Miss…Scan…dinavia*—he marked each syllable in the air with his hand—I'll sing it for you.

Marcel, using a cocktail napkin to wipe sweat off his neck, said, Please. Sing away.

You're ready?

I'm ready.

So here it goes:

Sexier than a California girl,
More luster than a Japanese Pearl,
With ooh-la-la above the Parisenne,
And any gal in the West End.
She's a six foot two, blond and busty,
Scandinavian.
But watch out.
She put the low,
In Oslo.
She crashed the stocks,
In Stockholm.
She killed all hope,
In Copenhagen.
She is the hell,
In Helsinki.

Henry stopped. His head lifted and he saw Paula and Denise were staring at him, amused. Then to Marcel, he said, That's it. What do you think?

Oh, well, yeah, Henry. I love it.

You *do?*

Marcel's head fell back, joyfully. He said, Good for you, son, and he smiled so that the corners of his mouth rose high to the middle of his cheeks. That song almost played on televisions around the world?

Henry blew air through his nostrils. He was tugging on his ear. He said, *Almost*, and stood straight up from his seat. Paula's graduation program, an anxious roll of paper, had escaped his jacket pocket, and lay on the floor. Henry stooped down for it and came up red-faced and off-kilter. He said, Everyone, I'm sorry, I have to go home.

From down low in the booth Paula stared at him. She looked like a child, the way she sat, of no more than twelve. She said, You're leaving, Henry?

I have to. Shaking with Marcel, he said, Nice to see you, sir.

Marcel clapped both his hands around Henry's. A superb piece of music, he said.

Thank you. Thanks. Well, I'll talk to you later, Paula. He kissed her goodbye, he embraced Denise. He couldn't wait to get out the door, away from the Mills', and Andy Powell. It was where he'd find peace.

THREE

The sun had already set, and Henry, seated under lamp light at his piano, drank from a small glass bottle of whiskey. He was trying to write a new song, but the dark sky of evening had intensified his fears. He was sure he was dying. Through his lungs up into his brain the cancer had spread. With chemotherapy they'd try to save him, but there was no chance of it. Life was over. Or else he was going to lose both his testicles. He'd never ejaculate again.

With two fists he struck the keys of the piano. Discordant treble notes rung out and in the quality of their sound was something murderous. Sweaty, hot, trembling, he put his face flat to the keys. At the next moment he could feel from inside his pocket the vibrations of his phone. He dug it out. Paula was calling. He stood back from the piano. He was so grateful to hear from her. His whole body felt warm. She was still at the Carlyle. Her parents had returned to their room and she'd gone to the lobby for privacy.

I haven't told them anything about the *bulge* in your back. Just like you asked, she said, proudly.

Thank you, Paula.

But my stepmother was after me. She was saying, Is Henry doing all right? and I told her, He's great. *Why?* and she said, I don't know, just seems not himself and—well, anyway.

Yes. Anyway.

What else did they say about your *bulge*, Henry?

Nothing more, really. They'll do a minor procedure.

Will it be painful?

A little, I'm sure.

He didn't mean to add layers to his lie. However, tomorrow, he'd tell her the truth. That was it. And he felt certain that the matter had been decided. He said, Come over, would you?

Come *there?*

Paula reminded him that it was the night of her graduation. She had plans to celebrate.

Right, said Henry. I don't know why I didn't think of that myself. His heartache returned.

Paula invited him to come out with her. Just to be asked made him feel better. Then she began to rescind her offer.

Or maybe I'll just come for breakfast tomorrow.

Tomorrow?

Maybe I should be alone with my friends tonight and I'll come in the morning and we can have a nice day. What do you think?

I don't know, said Henry.

Do you *want* to come tonight? If you want to, you should.

Walking his fingers along the black keys, he said, No. No, actually I don't think so. You go and have a good time. Come for breakfast in the morning.

Maybe around noon.

Sure. Come at noon, said Henry.

Okay. I'll see you then.

Putting down the phone, he lifted his head and saw his piano. My savior, he thought.

Playing did make him forget his sorrow. Soon his fingers took on great life, moving vigorously along the keys. Strong and loud, he felt every note in his chest. At one point his hands incidentally began to play the chorus to *Ms. Scandinavia.*

But *no, not that!* he shouted. *She crashed the stocks in Stockholm. She is the hell in Helsinki.* That's terrible. And it's over with. It never happened. You're not a jingle-writer.

He saw his own mad reflection in the long frame of the upright piano. With delirious eyes, he stared back at himself and said, Look forward. There'll be a future for you. You're not going to die. They'll cut it out and you'll walk away. Now put something down. Make some music. A song. A song for Walbaum.

Henry began to play, and within minutes he was lost in a new composition:

Faulk,
Old FRIEND,

Last month,
You called me,
Fifteen times,
In a single day.
Can't you take,
A hint?
I don't want anything,
More to do with,
You.

Faulk was not right in the head. He never had been. As recently as last month, messages, long, sentimental, remorseful, were coming to Henry via text at an alarming rate. It was not his first attempt to make amends for a particular misdeed. Undeniably, Faulk had wronged Henry, and he knew it. But he took offense when Henry didn't forgive him.

I don't care,
If it hurts,
I'm done,
With you,
For good.

Just shy of a year ago, Faulk appeared at Henry's door. Smelling oddly of gasoline and with dirt on his face, Faulk, once a handsome man, now bald and missing teeth, was agitated. Plastic bags full of junk encumbered his hands. He dropped them on the floor and went straight into the kitchen to make himself a vodka-soda.

Are you all right? Henry asked him.

All right? Henry, I'm on top of the world. Faulk, filling his glass with ice, said, I've got the *one.*

You're in love? Henry asked him.

Faulk said, No. Not love, but it is about a girl. She's a singer. Sonya. What pipes, what legs, you're going to love her.

Oh, I see. That's great.

Henry thought Faulk had given up on managing talent. He'd said he was going to begin a house-painting business.

I believed you were onto something,
With that idea.
For my own sake,
I was relieved knowing,
I'd never have to hear you say,
This one's going to be a star,
Or, that one's going to the top,
Ever again.

Since *All the Crazies Love Me* debuted on the radio, Faulk had been after Henry for help. One singer, and then another, and another, he insisted they be brought before Walbaum for a meeting. Henry was skeptical. He didn't trust Faulk's judgment of talent, and he would not be made a fool of with Walbaum.

Listen Henry, Faulk was circling his glass in the air, you have to listen to her sing. She'll make you drop. You'll want to call up your guy, Walbaum, and get a little *convo* going.

If your father, Lawrence,
Hadn't taught me to play piano,
I'd have told you no,
Way.

The Faulks had lived around the corner from Henry's family on East 92nd. His father, Lawrence Faulk, was a musician, a tall, imposing man, who kept a full beard. He wore thin black cotton pants, but no shirt, his chest hair dark and copious. Sheet music to Bach's *Minuet in G* sat open on the worn grand piano. In red ink at the top of the page he had written:

Make the Art. Earn your Death.

Henry and Faulk, both six years old, sat at the piano in the smoky room, the shades drawn. The furniture was all antique and stunk of mildew. Faulk's mother lived in Jersey. It was only he and his father there in the small apartment. Lawrence, lighting a cigarette, addressed them like prisoners.

Did you ingrates practice your scales?

We did, sir.

Don't lie to me.

It's the truth, Dad.

Lawrence smacked his son over the head. Henry, too. A couple of hopeless cases...how could I, just a man, make either of you any better? It's impossible. Agree or disagree?

Disagree, the boys said in unison.

Agree or disagree?

Disagree!

Lawrence would start the metronome at a slow tempo. For half an hour the boys would practice scales. Meanwhile, Lawrence would recline on a green divan by the window, smoking and reading the *Times*. Every so often his ear would tune into their playing.

Listen to the metronome. *Pah...pah...pah...pah pah...* If you can't stay in time, you'll never be any good. For crying out loud, feel it...feel it. Can you do that?

I'm sorry to say it, Faulk,
It was YOU your dad,
Was talking to.
I felt it,
Then, while you were busy,
Picking your fucking nose.
Well, your girl Sonya,
She couldn't sing,
And a thimble full of feel,
In your belly,
Would have told you,
As much.

Faulk brought Henry to meet Sonya. They took the A train to 181st Street to an apartment where Faulk and she had been staying, a dim-lit squalid place crowded with people. Sonya, with a bloody nose, reposed on the floor, a raggedy, sallow-faced woman, her head back, pinching her nostrils.

Henry had promised to listen to her sing. When the bleeding stopped, they went into the stairwell. Faulk came, too. She performed *Light My Fire*. Afterwards, Henry and Faulk went to stand under the George Washington Bridge. The sun was setting and the palisades were mollifying, a rich green color. On the cool river, with Sonya resting back at the apartment, Faulk nervously scratched at the many scabs on his forehead.

He said, You've got to help me, Henry. I need this. I know you could get her in front of Walbaum.

Henry thought Sonya's voice was only decent. He didn't see much hope for her. But he didn't say that.

My dad taught you how to play piano. We sat all those years in my apartment, like brothers. Now, what sweat is it off your back if nothing comes of this. What's it matter if Walbaum says, Nah, she's not the one. So what.

Faulk talked him into bringing Sonya by his apartment the next day to work on a song. They had stopped at a thrift-shop on 2nd Avenue and bought new outfits. Faulk had on a shabby black tuxedo with cummerbund and red bowtie, and a pair of patent leather shoes. He looked ready to tame a lion. Sonya, in a pink lace dress, her thin legs shaking, was so small and malnourished, all skin, bones. She was afraid that her nose would start bleeding, it had all morning. Faulk asked Henry if they could use one of his own songs.

You're such a great songwriter, Henry. We would be so honored if you let Sonya sing one of your own.

His old friend's compliments, manipulative and low-down, infuriated Henry. But he went into his songbook, anyhow. They worked all day. Sonya learned quickly. She had good energy. At least this was what Henry told Faulk when he was unable to find another positive remark to offer. Unfortunately, it encouraged him.

He said, So Walbaum, you'll give him a call and set up a meeting, right?

I can't believe I said,
Yes.

Before going up to Walbaum's office, Faulk told Sonya to take a walk around the corner to Bergdorf's and spray herself with some perfume.

You know how men get aroused on that stuff, he said.

Faulk should have gone with her. An inconsistent bather since childhood, he smelled awful, like b.o. In his black tuxedo, in front of F.A.O. Schwartz, he demanded Henry not back down easy with Walbaum. If necessary, he should put up a fight. He promised, if this worked out, he'd send at least $50,000 Henry's way.

Your mention,
Of 50 grand,
Exacerbated a feeling,
Of nausea,
Which only became,
Worse when we got,
Upstairs.

Walbaum, in a Mets cap and jersey, received them warmly. His assistant brought in espresso and croissants. On the leather sofa Faulk's legs were spread wide and his arm swung tragically around Sonya. Henry was in a chair in the corner. Walbaum, himself, stood behind his long glass desk, his hands on his waist, Trump Towers through the large window behind him. He discussed oral-hygiene. He said he was willing to do whatever it took to keep his teeth forever, pay whatever the dentist asked, stay off sugar, floss twelve times a day.

My grandfather's got these screw in incisors, see. I go to Queens to visit him last weekend, I find him on the floor with his head under a chair. I say, Papa, what are you doing down there? He says, I lost a tooth under the seat, a screw-in, it fell right out and rolled under here. It's caught in a dust bunny. I mean, forget it. I don't need that.

Faulk, chuckling insincerely, didn't know where to rest his hands. He moved them from his knees to his lap to behind his head. Walbaum saw all of his nervous motion. Henry was sure of it. The whole point of his dental claptrap was to give himself an opportunity to size up Faulk. No, the V.P. of Brass Records didn't waste a moment of his own time. Behind every action was a very real purpose.

Now what do you got for me? said Walbaum, turning a baseball in his right hand. This girl? We'd have to get you eating. The waif thing is out.

Faulk said, You can choose her diet, that's nothing to me. But we've had offers come in. Seven digits. Multi-record. You'd have to come forward with something big.

Walbaum set the baseball on his desk. Vivacious, happy, he winked at Henry. He said, It was a boring morning. Finally some entertainment. He took Sonya's hand, lifting her to her feet. Disconcerted, he looked her up and down. Baby doll, he said, let me ask you something...where do you see yourself in ten years?

Ten years? Sonya pulled on the hem of her skirt. Her smile was all-encompassing, her blue eyes vulnerable. She said, I don't know.

What she means to say is that life is unpredictable, Faulk interjected. His tux was newly pressed. However the red bowtie was crooked. He said, To answer your question, she sees herself at the top of the charts.

Hmm. Not a bad place to be, said Walbaum.

But then he made Sonya sing. And when she was through performing, not Henry's song, but *Goodbye Yellow Brick Road*—one of Faulk's last minute adjustments—Walbaum made everyone else leave. Adjusting his Mets cap, he thanked his old schoolmate for the pain he felt in his ass.

Every minute of my life is vital, you understand? This morning, you wasted my fucking time. Don't do it again.

Henry apologized to Walbaum.

Out on Fifth Avenue when he told Faulk and Sonya that Walbaum wasn't interested, a fight ensued. Faulk came at Henry, tackling him to the pavement. Henry was able to free himself. Faulk pursued him down the sidewalk. He was hysterical. He asked Henry how he could do this to his old friend.

You've been against me from the beginning. You don't want me to succeed.

That's not true.

It is, *too!* It is, Faulk insisted.

Henry let his hands up off the piano. Perhaps he *was* against Faulk succeeding. He really didn't know. He wouldn't think another second about it. The man repulsed him. He was a manipulator, a liar. Talk was all Henry ever got from him. Why would he want to keep their friendship going?

Perhaps my grandfather would be a better subject for a song, said Henry to himself. He's got to be.

Grandpa Itchy (*neé* Isaac, Itchala to his mother), unfit to care for himself, moved into an apartment down the hall from Henry, his mother and brother. A proud man, whose legs would still carry him, with a face which was thin and full-moon round, large ears, a macaw nose, Itchy, wearing only his red bathrobe, redid the work of the building's superintendent. He re-swept the floors, polished doorknobs, sorted garbage in the basement. It kept him busy. His kitchen was crowded with canned foods.

Tuna fish,
Sardines,
Pineapples,
Peaches,
Tomatoes,
Spinach,
Asparagus,
Lima, black,
And refried,
Beans.

Cans were stacked on the counters and blocked out the windows. Grandpa Itchy, preparing for the apocalypse, where he would not go hungry as he had during the Great Depression in the Bronx, made one trip out of the building each day and that was to the grocery store. Whatever cash he had on him he put into his cans. Since the death of his wife, Shirley, Itchy was coming apart. At one in the morning, in the hallway, he'd be mopping the floors, singing.

Henry came from his room in his pajamas. His mother, Edie, would hear the front door unlock and call to him from bed.

Henry? Is that you? Where are you going?

Grandpa. I can hear him in the hallway. I'll bring him to bed.

Itchy would have wet himself. Henry changed him into a new pair of pajamas. The old man having not lost his sense of shame would ask Henry to tell no one about his weak bladder. Henry would spend a few minutes before going back to bed organizing his cans. This cheered Itchy up.

Pie Fillers,
Apple,
Blueberry,
Cherry,
Pumpkin,
Were to be cleaned,
And stacked,
In alphabetical,
Order.

Same with the soup.
Chicken Noodle,
Cream of Broccoli,
Onion,
Minestrone.
Mom was worried,
When Grandpa's apartment,
Started to resemble,
A model of a city,
Populated by,
Many hundred buildings, like,
The GM Towers.

Itchy was severely depressed. His face was losing form. He slept all day. It was Henry's job to keep an eye on him after school. He often discovered Grandpa in the stairwell, his cheek resting flat on the tread, a toothbrush used for cleaning the floors in his right hand. Henry would tap the slumped man's back. Waiting to see if his head would lift:

And I sometimes screamed,
When it did.
Itchy screamed,
Back,
I'd lead him,
To bed,
That was no easy feat,
For Christ's sake,
The mattress,

Was surrounded by,
A damn sea of canned,
Salmon!

Henry, in his apartment, dropped this tune, declaring, But why's it all got to be so dreary.

He started up with another, recalling the day he and Paula met, when he saw her seated alone at a table on the back patio of Café La Fortuna, on West 71st. He asked if he could join her for coffee. For three hours they sat. That she turned out, like himself, to be a musician, injected immediate life into their conversation. She had a recital that night. Henry told her he'd like to come. She admitted that she was only page-turning for a piano player. Henry said he'd like to go anyway. And he did, complimenting her afterwards on a job well-done.

You were so quiet with the pages, he said, in the reception hall where parents, students and professors gathered. So perfectly quiet.

You think so? she said.

And the way your fingers pinched the corner of the pages—you didn't even have to lick the tips. What's your secret?

She said, My fingertips are my secret.

Henry took her hand and turned it over, inspecting them. Rough and hard-worked, he brought them nearly to his lips, squeezing, though not too tight. She asked him what he thought and he told her they were musically important fingertips, words which went right to her head. The next thing he knew she was leading him to a practice room on the floor above, locking the door behind them. They made love, in the dark, against a piano. Afterwards, she invited him to her apartment. He held her body all night. Soon after he wrote a song about it:

The subtle undulations of her shoulders,
The small radii of her nipples,
The slope of her ribs,
The short, light hairs of her neck,
And those which were dark,
And fell to shoulder length from her head.

Henry could recall her whole body in great detail. His powers of mental retention, that he could speak from memory about,

The smooth backsides of her thighs,
The curvature of her orbital bone,
The jagged lines of her palms,

had made her fall in love with him.

To see Paula play her violin was thrilling. *She* was thrilling. Waking to the sound of her violin strings vibrating through the apartment, Henry was overcome by the desire to make something great. On the piano he wasn't the *virtuoso* that Paula was on the violin, however, he knew how to write a song. And to do something truly inspired—why not me? asked Henry of himself. For as a younger man he'd had high hopes for his own life. He'd been determined to live *in* music, surrounded by great visionaries of the past, the present and future. He'd believed he would feed off their smarts, their energy. Rejected in America, but loved in Europe, identifiable by his music, his persona—above all else he would write great songs. In the years prior, he'd lost track of those hopes.

No longer.

What he decided on—his *great* project—wasn't a whole record, but *one* song that perfectly defined the thing he loved most: that is, New York City. And no matter how long it took or how many failures arose in the course of his trying, he would fulfill this mission. Maybe his thinking was narrow, foolish, quixotic, but he began work on the song. Meanwhile, he and Paula were growing closer. She was proud. When they first met, she thought his music ordinary. The way Henry spoke about his latest project, she changed her mind. Perhaps he was a smart man after all. She became less convinced of this over the next year when his song was never written. Henry blamed New York. He was too much in love with the city to write honestly on the subject. In truth, he felt so much anger. Greed seemed to be doing in its beautiful spirit, this time for good. Yet he couldn't make this clear in music, not with any real success. Eventually he gave up.

But what was happening here on the piano? It took him several minutes before he even realized that a song was coming together under his fingers. He stopped playing to write down words intermittently, the lyrics lacking the catchiness there in all his earlier writing. He sang:

Impotent, I blame the powers,
That have without conscience,
Watered-down the streetscape,
(I.e. he who has erected a,
Residential tower fast and cheap,
So as to fill it with new,
Paying residents,
Removed a century old deli,
For the sake of a bank,
Moreover, torn down historically,
Important theaters and,
Inserted chain-pharmacies in their stead),
They have demeaned our intelligence,
Street by street, and left,
My cock timid and confused.
We are all of us down to one ball. (x3)
Boom-bop-bop-bop-bop-bop-boom.

Arranging the song's structure, its piano lines and vocal melodies, his state was euphoric, though mentally unsteady. In a hard-thinking pose, with his hands spread wide over the piano keys and his face hovering just above them, he felt a strong pressure in his head. Fearing an aneurysm he grabbed his coat and went out into the night. The streets were empty. It was one reason he lived by the U.N., it became a ghost town after hours. And if every New Yorker went home to convalesce after a long hard day, then the silence here was equal to the ocean air recommended to the consumptive.

Henry brought all his new material to J. Van Gundy's, a bar on 40th. Just as more details could be gleaned about a song by listening to its recording, to play it live, for people, in a public setting, brought its own new understandings. Parts which worked and those which didn't became evident. Why this was true, Henry didn't know. It just was. And J. Van Gundy's had a piano. It wasn't a great instrument, but it was in tune, there wasn't a single dead note and the worn down keys felt good against Henry's fingertips.

He entered, the heavy front door swinging back, closing Henry in. From behind the bar Orion Doherty looked up.

Schiller, how goes it? he said.

The room was quiet and dark, fetid, warmer than the outside air, but it agreed with Henry. The same two men who drank here day after day, old with silver hair, they came from neighboring villages in Italy, were huddled drunk at the bar. Beside them a man with a short bourbon-wet mustache was asleep on his feet. No one else was present. Henry ordered a beer. His eyes were on the piano at the back of the room. He wanted to go to it and play his new song, to find out if what he had was any good. Certainly Orion would let him. He always gave Henry access to the instrument. All he had to do was ask.

Orion looked like Pavarotti or Francis Ford Coppola. Hirsute, corpulent, olive-skinned, he wore dark prescription sunglasses which took up half his face. His black hair was a tangled bird's nest on his head. He was discussing the slow state of business. For some reason Henry's thoughts shifted to his appointment at the sperm bank tomorrow. A kind of electricity moved through his spine. He rolled his shoulders backwards and forwards, releasing tension. He brought air into his lungs. At the moment of exhalation he saw Orion's middle-aged face, shadowy and thin-lipped, become excited. He was about to say something. Henry was so eager to play, however, he couldn't listen to another word.

He said, *Hey*, if it's all right, I'd like to use the piano.

The piano? Oh, yeah, sure, sorry, Henry. An injured look shot through his face, disrupting the balance of his sunglasses. Holding his hand out towards the instrument, he told Henry, Be my guest.

Henry went to the back of the room. The only light shone from a single brown bulb hanging above the piano. Henry could see Orion and the three men watching him. The long room had a sloping floor, and with fifteen feet between them, they appeared to Henry at a tilt.

So what are you going to play? asked Orion

It's a tune I started work on tonight.

Does it have a title?

He was about to tell him no, but the words *Castrated New York* were spoken. Around the bar all did silently nod their heads. The first notes of the song rang out. Hesitant in his playing, Henry missed notes in the opening verse. He was feeling better by the second. Reading from a sheet of paper, he sang:

I remember a time,
When New York City's newest structures,
Decayed gradually,

Now one site is hardly ever finished,
Before its parts are coming undone,
Unfortunately, the reproducing male,
Observing daily the structural depreciation,
Of his city,
Finds these days not even the insistent cries of fuck me,
Can get him to come,
No, the decaying visible world has yielded a body,
That knows better,
Than to release its seed,
To make children who will live in a city,
That is fast falling apart—the body wants to know:
Why consent to this?
We are all of us down to one ball. (x3)
Boom-bop-bop-bop-bop-bop-boom.

After finishing the song, Henry realized his rests between phrases had been inconsistent, and unintentionally so. He'd played the outro exactly like the intro, but he knew he didn't want to come in and out the same way. And the song needed a bridge. Tomorrow, in the afternoon, when he was through banking sperm, he would spend more time working on these things.

As it were, the problems which concerned Henry went unnoticed by those listening. Their reactions were overwhelmingly positive. The two men from the neighboring villages in Italy cheered. And to congratulate him on a fine achievement the man with the bourbon-wet mustache bought Henry a bourbon. It was Orion, standing at the end of the bar with his palms facing up and a look of wonderment on his face, who said:

You've been trying to write a song about New York for twenty years, right?

Two years, Henry corrected him.

Isn't this the *one?* Having heard many attempts at his song about New York, Orion had a sense of Henry's struggle. I think you've done it, he said.

Not for reasons of modesty but with the belief that he was assessing his own work honestly, Henry told him, Thanks, really. The song is just decent.

No! shouted the man with the bourbon-wet mustache. His shirt was buttoned low so that his stomach showed. His eyes were full of anger. He said, You're wrong. It's got something special, Henry. From the first notes, I heard it.

Well, thank you.

Don't *well thank you* me. I mean it, he said.

Orion sternly told him, You have a gem, Henry. A gem.

I appreciate your support, replied Henry. But it needs more work. Couple of days, maybe weeks, I don't know.

It's what you always say, went Orion. He'd come out from behind the bar. He stood within a foot of Henry and the piano. Resting his arms on the instrument, in the dim brown light, he said, *This* isn't any good. *That* isn't any good. What do you know about *good*, Henry.

The men from neighboring towns in Italy were staring at Henry. The smaller of the two, his skin was ruddy, and he looked ten years younger than his age, said, Why fight it, Henry? This is your song.

He is right, said his Italian neighbor. This is a great song about our city.

Do you actually think so? Henry addressed everyone in the room, his groin tender.

We do.

You don't think the verses could be a little stronger?

The man with the bourbon-wet mustache said, Orion, another bourbon for the jerk at the piano.

What about the chorus? said Henry, his right foot pressing down on the sustain. Do you think it has enough *umphh* to it?

It has *umphh*, said Orion, pouring him the bourbon. Setting the drink in front of Henry on the piano, he told him, You did it. Congratulations, Henry!

Henry wasn't convinced, but he let the subject drop. They made him play the song again. Four times *Castrated New York* was requested throughout the rest of the evening. At some point Orion locked the door and joined Henry at the piano, for he was an amateur pianist himself. The Italian men sang. As did the man with the bourbon-wet mustache. They went on into the early morning. And Henry did go home with the sun.

FOUR

At noon Henry woke. Light pierced through gaps in the old wooden shades. The succinct click of heels crossing through his apartment was what had roused him from sleep, though. Paula, it was her. Last-night's drinks were a powerful burning in his chest. He shouldn't consume liquor till his health returned to him. Dahl wouldn't approve. What about Henry? Did he approve?

I don't, he said, to himself. You have to keep your strength.

He could hear Paula stepping gingerly through his darkened bedroom.

Henry, she said, are you awake? Her voice was all gravel.

I am.

Good morning, she told him.

She went to raise the shades. A blue light swept into the bedroom, through the window a division of fire-escapes and low-rise buildings—a perfect June day. At twenty-one

Paula's face could absorb sleepless nights and still turn out beautiful the next morning. Yes, she was beautiful, in a loose white dress, and newly showered. Henry could smell jasmine strong on her body. Her black hair was damp. She'd been quick to leave home and come here, Henry acknowledged, with satisfaction.

How was your evening? he asked her, pulling on his bathrobe, knotting the belt.

It was good. And yours?

Fine, he said.

He told himself that he wouldn't talk about *Castrated New York*. He must speak of only one thing, his cancer. He said to her, Come into the kitchen. Let's have breakfast.

In the bright room he scrambled eggs, he made coffee, he toasted bread and took bottles of jam from the refrigerator, a carton of milk, and set them all on the table beside the plates and flatware and folded napkins which he'd likewise arranged. He even squeezed orange juice. Pouring egg yolk into a hot pan, he decided once breakfast was served he would tell her everything. That would be the right moment for it. You had to pick the one, and be *right*, he noted. You only had the one chance to say it the first time.

But Paula was speaking from her seat at the small round table behind him.

Henry, she was saying, I have to tell you something.

A hot needling sensation burst through him. Was she going to end their relationship? Some part of him felt certain that she would. Concealing the full load of his distress, he asked her, What's on your mind, Paula?

Loud enough to be heard above the traffic on the street below, Paula told him, I'm leaving Monday.

His eyes focused on her with relief. Grinning, he said, Leaving? Where to?

Paula, her gaze calm, her hands folded, said, To Berlin.

Berlin? *Really?* to Berlin?

I'll be staying in Europe for a while, I'm not sure how long. Maybe the rest of the summer, Henry.

What do you mean?

I'm going on the trip, she clapped her hands together.

You're leaving *this Monday?* for the whole summer? He was holding a wooden spoon to scramble eggs, and he threw it hard into the sink.

Henry—

This Monday?

It was the whole idea.

What *whole* idea? What are you saying?

The gift from my parents…it was arranged with Jeffrey Moss. I have three private recitals scheduled, first in Berlin this Tuesday, Vienna on Thursday and Paris, Saturday.

The pan was burning. Henry switched off the flame, averting his face from the rising smoke.

I'll be playing for the most influential people in the world. This is really *great* for me.

It *is*, but—

You're excited, aren't you?

I am.

These people will make my whole career.

That's wonderful. It is.

I know you're happy for me.

I *am* happy.

Because if you weren't...if you weren't happy for me Henry...

But I'm happy for you, Paula.

He had to stop himself from saying anything more. She must know the truth about his health. What was he even waiting for? Glancing down at her, he sensed the gravity of his mistake, each and every postponement of the truth, in the pit of his stomach. At once, he put himself in the chair next to her and scooped her hands up in his own. His eyes closed, he was going to say it all, right this minute.

Paula, he began. *Paula.*

What is it, Henry?

Paula.

Henry, are you okay?

Pushing back the shoulders of his robe, going, *Haaaah, haaaah, haaaah,* in a fight for air—it had dawned on him that Moss would be with her on this trip, he was hyperventilating—he said, It's just, I...I didn't realize...that...that you'd be leaving so soon. I...I...I have this procedure Monday to correct the *bulge.* They're going to suck fluids from my back. I have to leave soon and meet with the doctor.

Paula gently touched her lips, her conscience awoken. She said, God. Right. I hadn't even thought about that. You said it isn't serious. *Is* it serious?

Yes, it's serious. I mean...yes...it's not too serious, but *serious.*

How serious? she asked him.

I mean, you don't have to worry. It's nothing they can't fix.

It's just fluid?

Yes, he answered her.

And you can handle it alone?

I can.

You won't need me?

No, Paula.

He jumped from his chair, and went to the stove, took the pan, turned it upside down and whacked it twice against the garbage can under the sink. The eggs had been overcooked. Paula liked hers soft.

I'll make them again, he said.

You don't have to, Henry.

No, I will. I do have to.

From the stove he stared back at her, in fear. Quiet in her chair, Paula sat with her legs straight out and ankles crossed, her glass of juice tipped slightly forward below her upturned nose. And what was she thinking about? His gullibility?

Do something.

He said, Moss, aloud.

Again.

Moss, Henry spoke the name. His voice wasn't especially loud, but he was sure she'd heard him.

However, with her eyes blinking rapidly, Paula, lowering her glass of juice, said, I see what this is. I see it and I'm sorry, Henry. I know you want me at your procedure. I feel awful. I mean it, I thought it wasn't serious. But you're upset. She went to him, kissing his brow.

Why, she was pretending not to have heard him say *Moss*. She was. *She was*. Henry couldn't speak, he was sick. Paula—she was fondling his earlobe, saying, I'll come with you to the doctor today.

No.

I want to come.

You can't, said Henry.

I want to be with you.

You *can't* come, he said.

What can I do for you?

Nothing, Paula.

Nothing?

Just eat, he said. I have to go. I'm late.

Confused, she said to him, You're leaving so soon?

I have to.

Okay. If you have to. In a flash, her barren look turned to one of inspiration. She said, I'll wait for you to come back.

For her to spend the next hours here alone made no sense to Henry. Yet, standing next to Paula another second—he was afraid he'd act out with violence. He excused himself, he had to dress. In the bedroom, changing into khaki pants, a gray sweater, he shouted through the apartment, Paula, if you want to stay, *stay*. I'll be gone a while.

That's all right, he heard her say. I could use a rest. I was up late.

Fine. Do what you want.

His sperm-deposit was scheduled for two p.m. in the West 30s, near Penn Station. In the taxi his mind was reeling. She was back with Moss. She must be. Her teacher would travel with her to Europe. Henry would receive a letter in the mail one day stating that they couldn't be together anymore. She was in love with Moss. He was a better fit. He'd heard her say something like that before. Hadn't he? Because they did the same thing. Or were in the same field. Had the same interests. Bullshit. Henry was ready to move on, to release this burning sensation in his heart. He would find a new woman. He could do better. He must consider it.

Shouldn't I? he thought.

He felt that this person was not *him*. This paranoid man—who was he? Not Henry. It was Paula who made him behave like this. She ruined his mind. Made him tense and distrusting. That was her. Or, she brought out these qualities which were already in him. That is, she brought out the worst in him.

With his face in his hands, to himself, he said, You don't need her.

He noticed the taxi wasn't moving. No vehicles obstructed their path. Had the cabbie fallen asleep?

Excuse me, Henry said, can you drive? I'm in a rush.

But the cabbie, a gray-faced woman in her late 60s with long red hair, said, Open your eyes! We're here.

Henry looked up. It was true, they'd arrived at his destination. He apologized.

Just get out of my car, she yelled.

I am sorry.

Stepping from the taxi onto 7th Avenue, a tremendous brick building rose straight before him, its steel entryway gleaming white in the sun. On the 6th floor was the New

York City Cryobank. But it occurred to Henry that he'd seen this building so many times—and admired it, too—though never with the knowledge of what happened inside its walls, that there were men like himself who came in great desperation and sickness to store their sperm. Riding up in the elevator, with the escape-hatch in plain view and the shaft-to-freedom and its thick metal wires and near darkness stretching skyward, Henry wrung his hands. The doors opened and he stepped out the elevator onto a diagonal of linoleum-tiles, a wide-open space. Ammonia was strong in the air. As was the human emptiness of the New York City Cryobank. Where was everyone? The front desk, a white tome of Formica, and two gray sofas which formed a waiting area, were unoccupied. A sign on the desk caught Henry's attention:

To our Bankers, please keep in mind that it is only legal to store sperm for up to forty years in New York State. Thank you, the NYCC.

Henry's palms became wet with perspiration. Who could think so far ahead about reproduction? Madmen, tyrants, the mentally ill. Hopefully anyone who came here inquiring about forty years of storage had their files sent to the FEDs. But where was the staff? Leaning over the front desk Henry saw a computer up and running. A half-filled mug of coffee rested on an issue of *New York Magazine*. From a chair-back hung a white leather purse. Someone *was* here. But where?

Hello. Hello. Anyone. What's wrong with these people!

Without seeing the office blueprints he felt confident he could rob the bank and make off with everything in its vaults this minute. Who was keeping guard? No one. This was ridiculous. He checked the time on his phone. His appointment began five minutes ago. Weren't they expecting him? Perhaps Dahl had bungled the hour, told him two p.m. instead of one or noon. Just another stop on the doctor-go-round. But he couldn't simply leave. Today was Saturday. The bank was closed Sundays and the surgery was Monday.

The thought of not banking sperm passed through Henry, and fretful, he cried out, What's going on? Where is everyone? Come on.

A phone began to ring. Henry swung around and pursued the device on the front desk. Hovering over it, he watched its pulsing red light. Someone would answer. Someone. Anyone.

No one did. These people—unconscionable. Couldn't they do their jobs? *He* was doing his. He'd arrived on time. Hadn't he? Yes, he had. And he was ready to masturbate, ejaculate and pay the NYCC with a credit card for banking his sperm. What more did they want from him? He could take his business elsewhere. He might. He'd read about other banks, two, one in the Bronx, up by Fordham, another in Staten Island near the ferry terminal. Perhaps he should call one, or both, explain his situation. There was time, if he acted fast.

Instead he called Dahl. He got his service. Henry asked the operator if he could speak to the doctor. She explained how she could only tell Dahl to call him back, that that was her function.

Just make sure he knows it's an emergency. I'm at the sperm bank and there's no one here, and the doctor said he trusted these people—Henry was shouting into the phone—and I've been here five, ten, fifteen minutes, I don't know, a while, a long while, and where is everyone? Maybe the doctor has special information. And I've got to leave my sample here today because the orchiectomy's on Monday and... and...just have the doctor call me. Okay? Thank you. Thank you very much. It's Henry Schiller.

Henry hung up.

Put my life in the hands of these doctors and look what happens. Bunch of fucking idiots.

A woman appeared. Henry was ready to begin screaming. She apologized before he could say anything. She said she was the only person here today and that she had been afraid to use the bathroom ever since this morning, thinking someone might arrive, as Henry had, and find no one to greet him.

I'm so sorry, she said. Her hair was a pile of dark unruly curls, like some wig Little Richard might have worn. Her wide, brilliant smile neutralized Henry's anger. She said, Let's get you started.

She made Henry fill out forms. When he was through, she led him inside a clean bright windowless room. She drew blood from his arm. She asked Henry if the length of his sperm storage would be short or long term, or if he'd even thought about it. Without waiting for him to answer she recommended he consider the benefits of keeping his sperm in storage for the next forty years. He should understand it as a security policy. No matter what his sperm would always be safe.

If you don't mind my asking, why are you storing sperm today?

I've got testicular cancer.

Without giving into the sad expression on her face, she said, You think about what I've said, Henry. From a metal cabinet she removed a plastic cup, placing it firmly in his hand. For your semen, she told him. You've got every kind of magazine over there—she pointed to a large pile on a table—a television, DVDs. I'll be out there. You just take your time and tell me if you need anything.

Thank you.

She left the room and a strange, dark, hopeless feeling settled in Henry's breast. He removed his clothes. Naked and shivering, the air conditioning was turned to cold, he saw a large tub of petroleum jelly on the television. He went to it, removing the lid. He scooped a portion onto his middle and forefinger, sitting in a chair with good width separating his feet and opened a magazine, *Juggernauts*, to a photograph of a large-breasted woman receiving anal pleasure from a dildo. That would do. In his left hand he readied the cup. Shooting semen on the floor would be a grave mistake. So be careful, he told himself. Don't lose a drop. In two days this might be all that's left.

He now began to recall the terrible moment some three years ago with Colette Jacques, the sister of Bobby. Following the success of *All the Crazies Love Me* Henry had flown to Paris to see Bobby perform. He remembered how he'd planned to tour the city over his five days there but spent all but a few hours in Colette's bed in Le Marais. He'd thought, I'm having the time of my life. In Paris, with a beautiful woman, having great sex and such fine conversation, too. He went home to New York longing to see Colette again, unsure that he ever would.

Tu reviendras à Paris un jour? she'd asked him on his final morning.

Oui, bien sûr. Maintenant que je te connais, il faut que je revienne.

Tu es gentil, Henry.

Colette made no mention of visiting New York and Henry had been keen to her omission. He did want her to come. She was so kind and attractive. Her body had been lovely in his arms. It had been March in Paris, and freezing outdoors, they mostly stayed in.

Tu ne veux jamais te promener dans Paris avec moi. Te promener dans mon lit, il n'y a que ça qui t'intéresse!

But she had such a wonderful backside and shortly cropped black hair, and in the cold her smooth cheeks very quickly turned red. They went to see Bobby perform and Colette dressed for the Alps in black ski pants and a red wool sweater. She wore a shawl around her head and only her face went uncovered in the outdoors so that her light eyes alone were visible—they beamed full of deep emotion.

It was hard to leave you. I thought I'd never see you again, said Henry, to himself, and the issue of *Juggernauts* fell to the floor. I wonder still if it was better or worse that I did.

Colette had called one day the following summer from a payphone. She was in town for one night and desperate to see Henry. She didn't sound like the same woman. She was in a panic, disturbed. Henry had just moved into his apartment on 43rd and 1st Avenue. He was there entertaining his mother. But still, she could stop by if she liked. Colette said she'd be there soon.

Who was that? his mother asked once he was off.

Just a friend I made in Paris. She's coming over.

Edie had a look she gave her son when disappointed. Her lower lip came forward. On the left side of her face, the cheek assumed a heavy expression and the brown eyes looked on at him with the brow curved above. She said, Why do you have to see her now? I get so little time with you these days.

His mother had remarried and moved to Memphis where her new husband lived. She came to New York once a year to see her son and expected when they got together that she would have him to herself. Henry began to apologize. She was right. He should have met Colette in the evening.

She'd sounded so distraught.

Call her back.

I can't call her back. She was at a payphone.

Edie didn't say anything. But her discontent unnerved Henry. Colette arrived soon after and there was a man with her, a strong and hostile-looking person. In a long yellow dress, Colette appeared full of warmth. Her black hair was longer than when he had last seen her. She wore it back in a single braid. Her blue eyes were sorrowful. That wasn't unusual, they'd always been like that, it was part of their charm. She kissed Henry on both cheeks.

This, she said, is my husband, Luc. Luc, this is *Henri*.

Your husband? Congratulations, Henry smiled, disguising his unhappiness. I didn't know you'd been married.

Oui, she offered, revealing no emotion.

Colette came inside. Henry was ready to introduce her and her husband to his mother. Then he saw that Luc had remained in the doorway, his black eyes focused on Henry.

So *you* are the one? said Luc.

Henry said, I'm the *what?*

Colette held her husband's hand, and appeared to be restraining him from acting out with violence. She said, *Henri,* we won't be staying long. I am sorry. I had to come here today because Luc, he has told me for months that he must see your face, that he must look at you in the flesh and take in your image.

Henry and his mother exchanged confused looks. Colette hadn't moved. She was still with both hands on her husband.

Henri, she continued, when we were together, something happened, something for which I will never forgive myself, something I must apologize for, knowing you will still hate me for eternity.

Colette struggled to pull Luc closer to herself. Her cheeks were a dark red hue, her shoulders set back tense. In French, she reminded Luc of what they'd discussed on the way here: that this was only a chance for him to see Henry in person and for Colette to make her peace. That was it.

But Luc broke free of Colette and went straight out the door. Henry watched him leave, then noticed his mother peering apprehensively over her coffee mug at Colette.

Please, he said, what's this all about?

She said, *Oui, ecoute, Henri.* For five years Luc and I have been married. Long before I met you we decided to take lovers. Her chest steadily rising and falling, her hands at her sides with the muscles flexed, she said, When you arrived in Paris, Luc had just left on a trip with another woman. I had been so jealous. She was no ordinary person. She was Luc's great obsession. To get back at him, *Henri,* I removed my diaphragm, hoping you would impregnate me. Colette, in obvious distress, said, I didn't think it had worked. I felt none of the symptoms. But after two weeks, I came to see that I was so tired. And my hunger, oh my hunger was *so* strong. I went to have a test. It was true. You had made me pregnant, *Henri.*

Henry kept his hands over his face. This was too much to bear.

She said, I thought, What will I do? What *can* I do? Do I tell Luc? At first I didn't. I had an abortion. I lay in bed all day. My story was a stomach virus. But I couldn't stand dishonesty. I told Luc the truth. He was so angry...he didn't talk to me for a whole month, and—

Wait, cried Henry. Enough. Okay. God, I can't believe *you* would do this. I...I thought you were so kind, so sweet. I could have kept the memory. Why did you come here?

I told you, wept Colette, Luc was mad to see your face. I'm sorry we did. I'll leave.

She did.

Once gone, Henry's mother came straight to his defense. How was he supposed to know this would happen? she said. He was in Paris, spending a week with a beautiful young woman. A bit emotional sure—but that, too, could be attractive. She urged him to look on the bright side:

Honey, at least you're fertile.

Henry now climaxed, his semen shooting in the cup. Any softening of the muscles behind the eyes or weakening of the legs or slack-mouthed pleasure were ignored while he diligently captured his semen. A slight tickle in his nose let loose a warm tear. With his knuckle he wiped it free. Staring into the cup, though, he saw there wasn't much semen. Who knew how many sperm were actually swimming there? Certainly, by sight alone, Henry wasn't prepared to say. Yet considering this collection of fluid—there should be more of it than this. This—*this* was nothing.

Henry phoned Dahl immediately. Again he only got the doctor's service. He circled the room, pleading his case to the operator. He explained how he was still at the sperm bank and where certain things had improved—he'd located a staff member and he'd been given a room—however, he was still in trouble.

What exactly do you mean, Mr. Schiller?

What do I *mean?* He began to snap his fingers, searching for the words. Miss, said Henry, I've produced…a…a fucking half-teaspoon of semen.

There was silence on the line. After letting out a sigh, the operator said, Did the doctor tell you this might happen?

I…I don't remember. Would he have told me that?

Mr. Schiller, I'm really only an operator.

Henry squatted to the floor, though only momentarily, the position didn't suit him and he jumped up and paced the room. He said, A small child could produce more than I have.

Sir, again, I'm sorry. It was a young woman on the phone. Her tone was flat. She said, I don't know the answers to your questions.

Can I speak to the doctor? Please. I'll wait. I don't care how long. Just, I need to talk to him.

I'll call him again, she said.

Henry was put on hold. Sinatra's *My Way* piped through the phone. Henry, his pants still down, glanced at his testicles, but looked away just as fast.

Colette Jacques had rung his buzzer early the following morning. Henry had watched her from his window. There she'd been, all alone. Peach-skinned and with those heavenly blue eyes, she'd waved to him, a charming woman. Yet he'd decided not to let her upstairs. For them that was the end. He hadn't seen her since. But to this day, Henry regretted his decision. He still carried real feeling for her. Who knew what might have been that morning. He might have turned his back on some of the greatest hours of his life. And why? Because of *principle?*

Oh how *im*-fucking-provident, said Henry, to himself. How stupid.

Dahl was calling. Henry switched over, and before he could even greet him the doctor was explaining how, seminal fluids aside, his sperm count would be low because of the tumor in his testicle.

Though, once we remove it, Henry, it's very likely the numbers will go back up. This is normal. If you've produced any kind of sample at all you can rest assured your reproductive opportunities are secured for the future. All you need is one sperm.

Just one?

Just one, Henry...plus one egg...plus a little science equals new life. Now I want you to try and take it easy.

Henry said, Doctor, I'm losing it. I'm losing it. And you're not helping.

I'm sorry you think that. I've done everything I can for you thus far, Henry. What else would you like from me?

I'd like to be able to reach you when I need to.

You called my service. I called you back.

The delay was very long.

I'm sorry for that, Henry. I have other things in front of me. A whole life. Is there anyone else you've been talking to about this? A friend? A family member? You haven't been dealing with all of this alone, have you?

Henry said, No, doctor. Don't be ridiculous. I've got a lot of support. Thank you for your concern. I appreciate it—and he abruptly hung up the phone.

FIVE

In a taxi in traffic on 34th, Henry, feeling deeply unstable, tried turning his anguish into art. He saw that it all wanted to come out of him at once, every thought, in the honking and braking of the cars and the shadow of the Empire State Building, which loomed above, reminding him to forget his flagging health and Paula, and Moss, and think bigger than he'd ever in the past. The full crowds of people rushing along the sidewalks urged him to throw sharp elbows into a bridge for *Castrated New York*.

Writing on a New York City Cryobank receipt, the lyrics came quickly:

Lift up your chins,
Castrated citizens,
You didn't pay,
To have Upper Broadway,
Turned into a thoroughfare,
Which could be anywhere,

That would be the,
Developers of our city,
Those venal scumbag pricks,
And the politicians who suck,
Their dicks.

Henry carefully reread the lines. He realized they were too *something*. Certainly not *it*.

Placing anxious fingers to his head he searched for the right words. By the time he'd walked into his apartment he'd yet to find them. Paula called out to him when she heard the door slam shut.

Henry? You're back?

He cringed. He'd forgotten she'd said she would wait here for him. He didn't want to talk to her or see her face. He went straight to his piano. The bridge was being teased out in his head. The new lyrics did have a certain lyrical punch, however, the words *venal scumbag pricks/and the politicians who suck/their dicks* were too much. He had to find another, more tasteful, way to say exactly the same thing. He heard Paula approaching from behind. His shoulders tensed.

How did it go with the doctor? she asked.

Without facing her, he said, Fine.

He wanted her gone. A pile of blank sheet music sat on the piano, and he took those pages and began to straighten them. How would he get her out of here? He must figure a way. Slapping the sheet music to the keys, he said to her:

I can't be bothered. I have a new song that I need to work on.

He felt positive, hoped with all his person, that his words would penetrate to her most vulnerable parts. A little cruelty to get her out the door.

That wasn't what happened. Instead, with intense satisfaction, she cried, A new song!

Struggling for poise, Henry said, I wrote it last night, and I've already decided to bring a demo of it to Zachary Walbaum before my procedure Monday.

She said, Really? Zachary Walbaum?

Really. Him. And I'm sure this is *the* song.

Which song?

Which song? Which *song?* Henry mocked her. The one about New York.

She said, I thought you'd given up on that.

No, never given up, only put the song on hold for the sake of my sanity.

That makes sense.

I'm glad you agree, he said, feeling himself inch closer to a breakdown.

Paula, in an almost joyful state, pulled him by the hand to the piano. She said, You've got to play it for me.

No.

I want to hear it, she said. She fell into a chair beside the piano, crossing one leg over the other to show him she was a ready, eager audience. Smiling with half her face, she said, Play it for me. I've heard you talk so much about this song, how it would define your whole career, how people would come to know you by *it*. I'm deserving.

Paula, please.

I want to hear it, Henry.

No.

You're going to play it for me, she became severe now.

Ach. Fine, he said. I'll play you the goddamn song. Then I need to be left alone to work. I need total peace.

In a blithe voice, with the tempered blue light of afternoon filling the room, she told him, That's not a problem.

Pushing his tongue to the roof of his mouth to release spleen, Henry lowered himself onto the piano bench. He rested his hands on the keys. Ready to begin, he looked back at her. A wave of nerves passing through him, he said, Paula, there're things which still need to be worked out. I wrote the words to the bridge just ten minutes ago in the taxi home. I haven't even had the chance to sing them to music yet.

I understand. You don't have to explain anything, she said, taking a rubber band from her wrist and putting her hair back with business-like swiftness. I just want to have a feel for it. That's all.

Okay, fine. You'll get that.

Henry began. Playing through the first measures he explained to Paula how the intro was attempting to conceal the strong sense of indignation which came soon in the first verse by playing on these major and minor chords, back and forth. The whole part was trying to describe the mental state of a man, newly destitute, who alone on a June day in Times Square sees a place to sit, a bench on which he used to often rest but feels uncertain whether he's allowed to be there without buying something to eat or drink first.

Some iced coffee beverage or smoothie. You follow me, Paula?

Henry, she said, irritated, don't tell me what it's all supposed to mean. Just be quiet so I can hear the song. Okay? Now *continue.*

He did. Into the first verse, his right hand dropped from the playing altogether while the left worked low, discordant chords, steady sixteenth notes, haunting and abrasive. Perhaps it was too bleak an outlook for Paula. During the last seconds, in the reflection of the piano, he'd seen her stand from her chair and grab at her hair with both hands. He played on. But between those vocal lines:

Impotent,
I blame the powers,
That have without conscience,
Watered-down the streetscape,

and,

(I.e. he who has erected a,
Residential tower fast and cheap,
So as to fill it up with,
New paying residents,

he hit a handful of treble notes on the offbeat, semisweet but floating mysteriously in space, notes which appeared, then disappeared. Paula groaned. He gazed over his shoulder and saw her face was buried in the crook of her arm. She didn't see him. Turning back towards the piano, refocusing his efforts, he sang aloud:

They have demeaned our intelligence,
Street by street, and left,
My cock timid and confused.

Flushed red, Paula cried, Henry. *Henry.* Stop.

What is it? he shouted. He didn't want to break. Things were just heating up. Paula's chest was heaving, and her mouth was agape. She said, What are you doing? What is this?

What is *what?*

Countenancing a look, part confusion, part contempt, she sat down next to him on the piano bench. In a faint and gentle tone, one used on small children, she said, Henry, this song, it's *not* for Zachary Walbaum. I'm sorry. I have to be straight with you. He doesn't sell music like this.

She took the lyrics from the music stand. Come on. She was laughing at him. *We are all of us down to one ball.* What is that?

It's a metaphor.

For *what?*

Our city!

Henry, please. Her toothy smile patronized him. Pointing at the top of the page, she said, And what's this here? *Castrated New York?*

It's the song's title.

She looked terrified. Her eyebrows lifted towards her hairline. She said, You can't name a song *Castrated New York.*

Why not!

Because you *can't*, Henry!

She began to rock her head side to side, struggling not to disintegrate. And you cannot go to Walbaum with this. This is not your great song about New York, and it's completely un-salable, and he'll know it the second he hears it.

This song already has fans, Henry barked.

Really? Her look showed she was ready to believe him. She said, What fans?

A couple of warm-blooded human beings, that's who. I went to the bar last night and—

Oh, *oh*, no, she began running her fingers in the air, as if moving them up and down the neck of her violin, something she did when she was worked up, you mean those drunks from J. Van Gundy's? Is that what you're trying to tell me? Henry, those guys love *everything* you do.

Okay, just get out of here! he shouted. Go. Leave.

You're lucky I'm here, Henry. You're lucky you have me. Look, I know you don't like to hear any of this, but—

Henry cut her off. Enough. Enough! he yelled. He rushed to the front door, his wounded steps pounding the floor. Unbolting the lock, he turned to face her. He said, *Leave!*

Paula had followed him to the narrow entryway. She said, Come on, Henry, please. I'm just trying to help.

Henry said, Bullshit. You just can't admit I've written a great song. You want to keep me down. I know how you think.

Henry, please.

No, no, you're in competition with everyone. Including me. Pulling open the door, he cried out, You're just a sick fucking bitch, and that's all there is to it!

Her eyes enlarged, hyperthyroidically. Without saying another word she rushed past him, out of the apartment. Henry slammed the door and went back to work.

Within seconds, and seated at his piano, he began cursing her name. Because really, what does she know? I'm the one who's written a hit song. And she's five minutes out of college. A child. Never supported herself a day in her life.

The shortness of his breath further excited his nerves. He demanded he pull it together and reset his focus. The song was, he told himself, the single important thing in his life. Pounding his fist to his breast, his eyes lit up. His face was wet. Taking a harsh look at the piano, he jumped to his feet and rushed to the window. In the past when they'd argued, Paula had gone to stand in front of the building to cool down. He got his head all the way outside and searched left and right. He didn't see her anywhere. He put on shoes and went to look for her. He searched Beekman Place, and a bench on 57th Street at the river, places they often went together. The air was getting cooler, it was after five. He couldn't find her. In front of the U.N. he called and she didn't answer. He left no message. But forget it. He didn't need her.

Upstairs he fixed himself a vodka. Bent against the counter, his strength decreasing, he drank it down. Suddenly, more than to feel drunk, he wanted to call his mother and father, to have their love. He could do that. He hardly understood what kept him from it. He wasn't an orphan. Not yet. They would come to him, they could be here tomorrow, if he called. If he asked.

He lay down flat on the kitchen floor. Staring at the shadowed ceiling he saw his father out on the avenue hailing a taxi. His mother was there too. His parents, they were escorting him to the hospital. His mother helped him into the yellow car. His father told the driver the address. And Henry sat between them, a child once again. Seeing his parents in the waiting room brought a tear to his eye. He dabbed it with the back of his hand. Then another fell, because they'd be there when the anesthesia wore off and consciousness resumed. They'd talk to his doctor. A great relief, thought Henry, who didn't want to confer with another MD as long as he lived. His parents would take him home, nurse him through his treatment, make sure he had food, and warmth, money.

I could use a loan, said Henry, to himself.

His eyes, red and glazed, closed against the day. He could almost recall the figure of his last bank statement: $194.05. Or was it $149.50? Either way, he was closing in on zero.

Henry steadied his shaking hands on his forehead. He wouldn't think about his parents. Dr. Penelope Andrews, on the other hand—she'd been so sympathetic to his condition. Dizzy, the gray filter subduing his vision, unable to look at his piano, she'd welcomed him into her office and had sex with him. What a wonderful woman, he thought. She was there for me. She had such a nurturing character, and so much love to give. So warm. She was lovely. I loved her, said Henry, his throat aching with emotion. I really think I might have loved her. She was a special woman. Rare. Charming. I should call. She'd come and spend the night. I could tell her everything that's happened. She'd want to know. Never had anyone taken such an interest in my problems. Her insights were excellent. She had a way of seeing through to the truth of my every thought. Ahhh. She was something. Something else.

With his head beneath the door to the old stove and the refrigerator dully humming nearby, he said, I'm going to get her on the phone.

His stiff, nervous fingers began to dial. He hadn't forgotten her number. There'd been a stretch of months when he used to call her four and five times a day. The phone was ringing—once, twice—he hung up.

Do I really want to see Penelope?

Waiting a second, he then dialed again, and hung up just as fast. His back flat to the kitchen floor, to himself, he said, Remember, she was the one who stopped talking to you. What makes you think she'll answer your call, let alone see you? Henry scratched under the band of his pants till the skin ached. He reckoned that Penelope Andrews would answer, though. Why? Because if he were calling, it meant he needed her. Because he was desperate. And that was how she liked him.

He dialed again. The phone was ringing. Come on, come on, come on.

He got her voicemail and hung up. Banging his head again and again on the kitchen floor, he said, What the hell does Paula know about songwriting anyway. Nothing. She's never written a song. She wouldn't know how to start writing a song if she tried. And I've *sold* a song. I've made a living by it. That's what *I* do. That's my place of expertise. I have a reputation. And *Castrated New York* is a groundbreaking work. And it *must* get to the people.

At the next moment, he called Zackary Walbaum. His heart rate wasn't under control by the time Walbaum answered.

What's doing, baby? How you been?

Henry looked around in alarm. He was still on the kitchen floor, no place to conduct business, and he hoisted himself to his feet.

It had been months since they'd last spoken. But their conversational tone was always familiar. After all, they went back to grade school. Of course, Henry knew not to over-romanticize their relationship. Walbaum's Porsche was imported from Germany and he was after the next new thing. This was business.

Why in god's name are you calling me on a Saturday?

Henry paced back and forth through the kitchen. His free hand clutched the back of his head. He could hardly control his volume. He said, I've got the song for you, Zachary. Wait till you hear it, you'll be blown away. I want to play it for you tomorrow.

Tomorrow? Tomorrow's Sunday.

So what.

So, can't we do it Monday?

Going away, Zachary.

Where to, *jail?* You in trouble?

I'm fine, he said. I'm absolutely fine.

Walbaum was the last person he'd tell about his poor health. His old schoolmate had even warned him against it one evening at a small party in honor of Bobby Jacques at the Rainbow Room. Sixty-five stories above Midtown and staring out over Manhattan, Walbaum had told Henry that a certain music label CEO had made it public he was fighting Hodgkin's Disease. Walbaum had said to Henry:

My friend, here's a business tip on the house...Never show the enemy any sign of physical infirmity. No one puts their money on a gimp horse.

However, once again now, Walbaum was asking him what was wrong.

He said, I've never heard you sound like this.

Leaning in the kitchen doorway, Henry considered how he'd never been admonished about hiding his romantic woes. He said to him, Do you remember Paula, Zachary?

Remember *her?* Walbaum began to laugh. Ambitious little thing almost convinced me to make a classical record. Christ, you know, she'd have gotten me fired. How she doing?

She's leaving me, said Henry.

What? I'm sorry to hear that.

Gripping his sweaty phone tight, Henry said, I didn't mean to discuss any of that. I want to talk music. I said I have a song for you.

Baby, I hear you. And since you're so down, let me give you a little good news. Bobby Jacques—she's up in a studio in Montmartre, and she's in need of songs.

Really? Henry's eyes flashed with excitement.

Is yours something she could use?

Henry, letting go of the dark feeling inside him, said, I practically wrote it *for* her.

I trust you mean it.

I do.

Good, said Walbaum. You'll meet me at Greengrass. Tomorrow. Twelve-thirty.

That's great, Zachary.

Tell me, what's the title of this song?

The title? said Henry. Recalling Paula's criticism, he said, It's *C.N.Y.*

C.N.Y.? Sounds like a forensics show.

It's an acronym, *all right*.

Look who's so smart.

Like *P.Y.T.* or *O.P.P.*, Zachary. Those were big songs.

Okay. So what's that stand for, your *C.N.Y.*?

I'll tell you over breakfast.

Henry hung up, charged with frantic energy. Forget Paula. Walbaum would see him. And though *Castrated New York* wasn't the song for Bobby Jacques, it was brilliant still, and as soon as Walbaum heard it, he'd think the same, and want to do something bold with it. Yet it had to be finished by morning. Thank god the hour was early. He could do it.

I must.

He went to brew coffee. Outside the kitchen window, an early summer afternoon, and the sky would still be light for hours. He boiled water. Staring at the kettle, he saw a great future for himself. His whole body felt powerfully alive. He let out a laugh and took his coffee to the piano, diving into work. He played passionately. At one point, apoplectic, he stood and kicked over his piano bench, like Jerry Lee Lewis, his body trembling tensely over the instrument. Sweat stung his eyes. His fingers pounded hard against the keys so that the tips smarted. On top of the instrument was a lamp and a photo of Django, and it all shifted closer to the piano's edge. Henry, his mind having moved far inside itself, didn't notice that they were in danger of falling. Playing *Castrated New York* over and over again he made slight changes to the feel, the rhythm, dropped notes, added rests, shortened the intro, doubled the last chorus. His mind pushed around those last obstructions, shoved them furiously aside, he could taste how close he was to a symmetry of notes, of feeling and sound. Minutes later he looked up to see Django fall to the floor. The lamp was set halfway off the piano. The keys were damp with sweat, the bench overturned behind him. He lifted his hands from the keys and stood back. The bridge, he realized, was finished. The intro and outro were finalized, the song done. It was time to record. He could barely keep his hands steady long enough to adjust the levels of the four-track. He managed to get tape rolling. While he played his piano and sang aloud with a microphone set on a stand to the right of the instrument, all he could think was how Walbaum was going to love the song. Here was what he'd been waiting for. Henry's great number about New York City, after so many years, was finally written. It was the *one*, a hit. It would define him, *Henry Schiller*, from now unto forever.

SIX

The next morning, awoken by the sound of a helicopter flying nearby over the East River, Henry got out of bed and went to wash up. His body felt worn by exhaustion. His skin had a kind of thorniness to it. Brushing his teeth, he began to think of Paula, admitting to himself, with pity in his heart, that the violin was her life, and that she had no other *life* to speak of. Her deceased mother was still pressuring her to succeed. And her father was so supportive, one had to be suspicious of that, too. He dried his mouth with a towel and went into the bedroom, dressed in his dark linen suit, a black tie and white shirt, acknowledging how Paula couldn't help another person in a crisis. She wasn't good at expressing love. She didn't know how, or what it was, to be warm and that was very sad, thought Henry, locking the door and heading out into the city. Because even if Paula did know a good song like *Castrated New York* when she heard one, she'd never have real love.

He sighed. Poor girl.

The streets had the quiet-emptiness of a Sunday morning. The cars were few. Henry felt he had the city to himself. The abandoned air of Midtown didn't stop these sympathetic feelings for Paula from flowing. He wondered, Could the achievement of all her aspirations make her feel fulfilled? Would she be happy? Or would she regret having never truly loved another person?

It would be her greatest sadness, Henry answered for her.

At the fountains of Columbus Circle, his grief for her nearly overcame him. He stuck his hands in his pockets, tightly gripping the fabric of his pants. He had to warn her, he thought. Tell her not to ignore the many riches of life. He couldn't give up on her just because times were difficult. *Life* was difficult. And good things came with great difficultly. Didn't they? But even if they *didn't*.

He had a half-hour before meeting Walbaum. Paula's apartment was close. He'd stop by there. No doubt she was home, practicing. Each day began for her at five a.m. She played till eleven. He wouldn't call to tell her he was coming. He'd surprise her by ringing her buzzer. And if she wouldn't let him in, he'd make his feelings known from the sidewalk. He couldn't help smiling.

You are a fool,
Henry.
She's fucking him.

Taking a handful of his dark hair, he said, to himself, But you don't know that for sure.

Yes, you do,

sang the voice inside his head.

You've never,
Not known,
Only decided,
To look,
Away.

These thoughts so painful, his balance began to give out. Holding himself up against a red brick building, he decided that what he really needed was a drink. Before saying hello to Walbaum, a drink. He couldn't sit and have a proper meeting when he felt like this. How could he show any enthusiasm for his work? How could he form full sentences?

He went into a tavern off Amsterdam, two blocks from Barney Greengrass. He had ten minutes to spare. It would be one drink then.

Henry could remember the tavern having been here all his life. But there was a bad air about it, and he had never been inside. A black curtain ran straight across the window at the front, so that you couldn't see in from the sidewalk. It was darkly lit. There was sawdust on the floor. An older man with a white mustache and thin silver hair which he combed with his fingers stood behind the bar. He gave Henry a strange look the moment he stepped through the door. The bar had opened only recently, but a half-dozen people were already seated on stools and drinking. No one spoke. Large, rectangular tinfoil containers of eggs and bacon were on a table in the corner, giving the room a peculiar odor. Above them was a sign which read:

Come in and enjoy breakfast on us.

Henry ordered a vodka rocks and sat down in the booth furthest to the back. Looking at his hands, red and shaking, the thought of Moss and Paula's bodies together further enflamed his face. To himself, he was saying, They'll spend the whole summer together, traveling through Europe. And where will you be? What will you be doing?

Labored and wispy, air passed through his lips. It felt like he had to work his own lungs in and out, that they wouldn't operate on their own. He pulled open the top of his shirt, the second and third buttons popping off and rolling across the table to the floor. He didn't bother retrieving them. There was a man seated two tables over. Henry could feel his gaze. Clearly this man, whose black suit had a large tear at the elbow of the right arm, wanted to talk. Henry drank faster. He had to go. He would be late to meet Walbaum if he didn't hurry. The man kept rapping his knuckles on the table, groaning. His face was unshaven. Around his eyes was a sweaty glow. He had a tie that was perfectly straight on his neck. But, like his suit, it had a tear. There was a little bit of blood around the nails of both thumbs. His hair was long in the back, greasy. Henry noticed a full bottle of red wine on the table before him. It was more than halfway finished. The man sighed after every sip of wine, but proudly, letting himself be heard. Then, of a sudden, he said, to Henry:

I can tell you're smart.

Henry looked up at him, smiling weakly.

You walk around this city, you don't meet smart people. Not many. You know what I mean? Well, I know a smart guy when I see one. I'm a driver myself. Limousines. Name's Marshall Fleming. Let me guess, you're a doctor.

A musician, said Henry, irritated. He didn't have time for conversation.

A musician, said Fleming. And guitar's your instrument?

Piano.

Fleming said, Hmm, and he came up from his chair, took his bottle of wine and sat down at the table next to Henry's, but across from him. He refilled his glass, spilling on the table. He stared at Henry, excitedly. He said, Let me ask you, sir, have you ever spent a night on a park bench? Actually, it's a trick question. Because you can't. The police force you to move. It's a problem. But I blame myself, really, and that's why I'm drunk. Have you ever slept in Riverside Park?

Henry shook his head no.

One of the men sitting at the bar turned to Henry and said, Don't listen to him. He tells a different guy the same story every day for the last week.

Get a job! the bartender shouted at Fleming.

Do you think I like being out of work? You think I want this! When Mr. Kelly pushed my wife down those stairs, do you think it didn't hurt like hell? He said, My one daughter, Carolina, she went out and became an…an…escort. No, no never mind. Forget I even started telling you about that.

Henry nervously drew his glass to his chest.

It's true, I'm horseshit. And Dana, my wife, she's smart. For one thing, she grew up rich. But she doesn't have a heart. She's generous, but cruel. If she'd just...aw Jesus. Why am I even telling you any of this? There's no point. I'm nothing but horseshit.

Amen, said the bartender.

Fleming spit on the floor. And what if I am? So what! Did you know I stole Dana's ring and hocked it for booze? And the pearl earrings her father bought her for her sixteenth birthday—sold them off, too. Drank it. And we've got a couple of kids. Dana spends so much time taking care of them. She's always sick. So I drink. And it makes me feel worse. That's why I do it. Not to feel happy, but miserable. My wife, she is smart. But she's always fighting with the landlord. Excessive pride, mmm. And she's fiery, and stubborn. Don't tell her she's not a strong woman, you'll pay with your life. Then after Mr. Kelly insulted her, and she got in his face, he gave her a shove down the stairs. She went tumbling, god. Nothing broke, but she was so depressed afterwards. All she did was sleep and sleep. And you know, when we first met, her husband, Edward, had just died. She said to me she would never love a man more than Edward. He beat her up, too. Still, compared to Edward, she says I'm worse. She was left with all these kids though, living up on Amsterdam. That's where we found each other. She had nothing, not a cent. Her family wouldn't even talk to her. Didn't matter, because she didn't want their handouts. My own wife had just left me. She disappeared one day, leaving me with our daughter. Carolina was about thirteen then. I married Dana because...

because you see a woman like that living with nothing and you want to help, right? She's so smart, but things weren't going right for her. I thought, Step in, do something. I was shocked that she married me. Truth is, she didn't want any part of me. Except I said I would take care of her. And for years and years, I did everything for her. I gave her a decent life. Then I'm driving the boss' limo one day and ran it into a lamppost. I was drunk, you know. It cost me my job. I lost my license. There was a short stay in prison. Can I tell you, I don't know how we're paying our rent these days. My daughter, Carolina, she and Dana, they don't get along. Dana's got a nasty temper. She'll snap and look out! But Carolina had to drop out of school and get a job, to make money for the family. She loved it, too, going to class, learning. Absolutely loved it. She doesn't have a diploma, though. And what do you think you can earn without one of those? Minimum wage. But a person can't live off that. Not in this city. It's not possible. Unless you work a hundred hours. And then you die from exhaustion. We were all going around hungry. My wife was becoming more and more sick, and angry. She looked at Carolina one day, and said, Come with me, now. See, there was a man around the corner who did this thing for young women, set them up with men, you know. My wife arranged for them to meet. That doesn't make her a bad woman. She was just losing her mind, from hunger. There were the kids to think about. Something had to be done. I saw my daughter go out this one night. She didn't come back till three in the morning. She tossed a stack of bills on the table next to my wife, and went straight into her bedroom. Dana went in after her. They didn't come out all night. I peeked in on them, though, and saw Dana with Carolina in the bed, and she was holding her.

Fleming covered his mouth, turning his attention at the ceiling. He reached for the bottle, refilling his glass. Henry was about to tell him he must leave. Fleming spoke first.

My daughter couldn't face coming home every night from work. She moved in with a friend, on the West Side, Harlem. That's when Mr. Kelly and my wife got into it. I've known the guy, too, and never thought he was all that bad. But he shows up at our door one evening. Dana answered. I could hear them quarreling. Mr. Kelly was saying, I feel so much better now that I don't have to live upstairs from your girl. You keep that whore out of the building. My wife… now I've seen her get mad, but not like this. We keep a baseball bat right inside the door and Dana, she took a swing at Kelly. But Kelly's a strong guy. He grabbed it out of her hands and gave her a shove. She was standing right at the top of the stairs, and went tumbling down. I had to take her to the emergency room. She was all right.

Fleming let out a hard cough. He said, The day after the incident with Mr. Kelly I called up an old friend, Thompson. A good guy. If you knew him, I mean a classy person. I told him what had been going on with my daughter and wife. I nearly had him in tears. He asked me what my last job was. Limousine driver, I said. By that time I'd gotten my driver's license back. He said he usually drove himself around but that he'd hire me on in the role, as a favor. I was so glad.

Fleming took a long drink from his glass. He wiped his mouth, and said, My wife, she was over the moon. She used to treat me like garbage. Now I was a king. I came home that first day of work and she had a meal waiting for me. Steak, wine, the works. She took my coat at the door, hung it on the hook. Her tone was respectful. After dinner, she gave my back a rub. I'm not sure if she'd ever done that before. The next morning I found my shirt had been pressed, my slacks, too. There was breakfast on the table. She told the children how wonderful I was. Then I came in later that day and she was sitting with her girlfriend, Doris. I can't tell you how many times I'd overheard her talking with this Doris about how awful I am. All my shortcomings, and everything she lost when her husband, Edward, passed. Not this day, though. Dana, she was going on about how terrific I was. She was praising me, as a husband, a father. Then I came out from where I'd been hiding, and I said, Girls, I heard all that. And Dana said, Well, it's true—and we all laughed. And my wife was so happy. I was happy. I think for the first time in our life together, things were working out.

Fleming paused, inspecting the wine bottle. Conserving what remained of it, he poured only an inch into his glass. Watching the man, in fear, Henry's phone began to ring. His heart skipped. What time was it? Behind the bar, a cable box on the television showed it was 12:30 exactly. But Walbaum wouldn't stick around for Henry. How had these ten minutes passed so quickly? He had to get out of here, away from this man.

I hope, said Fleming, taking Henry by the wrist and giving his hand a firm pat, I hope I'm not making your head ache. Because for that one day, I was really on top of the world. What a feeling I had in my heart. Life is good. Life is good. I kept feeling that it was true. Then wouldn't you know it, not twenty-four hours later, I screwed it up. I don't know how it happened. But there I was, on the sidewalk. Thompson's car was wrapped around a pole. The engine was on fire. I failed the breathalyzer. And my daughter, she had to bail me out of jail. I haven't been home since. My wife is probably looking for me. I've been sleeping in the park. But who should feel bad for me?

No one's going to feel bad for you, said the bartender.

All the men began to jeer. Some just stared, in awe of Fleming.

Why should your hearts go out to me? asked Fleming, standing up from his chair. I ought to be put in the electric chair. I'd like to get the guillotine. Yeah, chop off my head and when you see it come off you can laugh at me because there's my head on the goddamn ground.

Ahh, shut up, said the bartender.

You think your wine makes me happy, you bastard. Well, I was looking for misery and I found it. So there.

Henry checked his pocket. There was the demo to *Castrated New York*. He took his last five dollars and put it on the table for Fleming. He said, It's all I have. I'm sorry. I'm in a rush.

Henry could feel his phone ringing again. Fleming was vehemently scratching at his beard. He said, I don't want your money. Just help me up. Help me out of the bar, please.

All right. Fine. Sure, said Henry.

Walbaum was going to kill him. Yet now Fleming was begging Henry to take him home, over thirty blocks up Amsterdam. Henry said no, however Fleming tripped, falling to the floor of the bar. There was sawdust in his oily hair. Henry picked him up. He could not refuse him. On the avenue, he hailed a taxi. The ride took under five minutes. Fleming lived in a large brick building. He couldn't get out of the car alone, and had to be hoisted onto his feet and supported inside. They rode upstairs in an elevator.

Fleming was saying, You'll come inside with me, won't you? Please, come in. Just let me introduce you to my wife. I'll tell her you're my new employer. You would do that for me? Tell her you've given me a job, with a better salary than the last. Oh, she's going to kill me. I hope she gives me a good sock to the face. I want that. God, let the kids be out. I don't like them to hear their mother get so upset. Just tell her you're my new boss, please, and that you're paying me $25,000-a-year salary. Okay? Please, just tell her that. Please, would you? Tell her you had to take me away these last days, for training. That's why I haven't been home. You'll do that for me, please?

They were standing in a long hallway right outside Fleming's door then. But Henry said, I'm sorry. I can't help you anymore. I have to go.

SEVEN

Henry filed recklessly down the stairwell. He had to get outside, into the open air. But where did that man come from? Ach, don't think about Fleming. Not him. Not Paula. Not Moss.

He resolved to go straight to Walbaum's apartment. What use was there in calling him on the phone? He'd have to go to his door, get down on his knees and plead. That was it. He had no other choice.

Walbaum lived in the West 80s, off West End Avenue. Henry wasn't far. What could he tell Walbaum that would make him understand? Would the truth be powerful enough to convince him that he'd meant no disrespect by standing him up? Henry wondered, the muscles in his face convulsing. Walbaum's doorman led Henry inside the lobby and asked him to wait while he rung up to the apartment. Over and over in his head Henry was singing:

Unfortunately, the reproducing male,
Observing daily the structural depreciation,

Of his city,
Finds now not even the insistent cries of fuck me,
Can get him to come,
No, the decaying visible world has yielded a body,
That knows better,
Than to release its seed,
To make children who will live in a city,
That is fast falling apart—the body wants to know:
Why consent to this?

Excuse me, sir?

Henry gazed up at the doorman, whose hat, like his pants, was a few sizes too large. On his face was a concerned look. The doorman said, Is Mr. Walbaum expecting you, sir?

We're old friends, Henry answered.

Mr. Walbaum told me you should leave.

Henry didn't move. He could still smell Fleming's foul scent in his nostrils, a mix of wine and sweat and dirt. In a firm voice, he said, That's because we're arguing, and from time to time that's how it goes with *old* friends. Can you buzz him again and let me speak?

The doorman wasn't a day over eighteen. He deliberated a moment. By the heaviness of his expression it was clear he thought an answer of yes would cost him his job. This and the nervous rapping of his fingers on the switchboard was enough to make Henry lose patience. He told the doorman he'd call Walbaum himself, on his own phone. He dialed. The phone rang.

A few seconds passed and the doorman said, Mr. Walbaum isn't answering, *is he?*

Henry said, Let me call again. His heart filled with pressure. He was determined to get upstairs. He told himself, You'll play your song for Walbaum. You have to. After two rings, though, it seemed Walbaum wasn't going to answer. Henry saw only one option for himself and without delay he made a run for the stairwell. The doorman called for him to stop, but Henry swiftly climbed the stairs. Walbaum was up on the twelfth floor. By the time he'd mounted every flight, Henry thought he'd drop dead. His face was crimson, his mouth hung open, his legs felt like they'd give out at any moment. The doorman was waiting for him upstairs. Henry held both hands in the air, as if he were going to submit, then began to bang on Walbaum's door. He kicked at it, too.

Zachary! he shouted. Zachary, open the door. Let me in, goddamnit!

Sir, please. Restrain yourself or I'll be forced to call the police. Now, you have to leave.

Henry, exasperated, cried, Call the police. I don't care. I won't go until I've seen Zachary.

He screamed Walbaum's name again and again. The doorman had a phone, and said he was now dialing 911. Then Walbaum appeared, his face concealed behind a narrow crack in the door. The doorman apologized. He said there was nothing he could do. He'd tried to stop him. Walbaum said, Forget it, and reached for Henry, yanking him violently by the sleeve into his apartment. He shook him by the arm, said, *You.* You waste my fucking time.

Henry, with bowed head and a pounding heart, tried to state the entire events of his morning. Walbaum wasn't listening. He walked away from Henry, leading him into the kitchen. He wore a gray running suit. He was drinking a kind of health drink from a Mets souvenir mug. He thought Henry's story impossible.

I'm telling you that's how it went, Zachary.

You're lying.

Henry looked at the floor, as if he might get on his knees and swear to him that every word he spoke was the truth. He shrank a few inches to Walbaum's height, holding out his hands to him, said, I know you're angry, I understand. It's Sunday. I *have* wasted your time. I swear, though, I haven't lied, not once. I want to play you my song. It's why we're here, isn't it? Come, let me play it for you. Let's go to your piano.

However, Walbaum's pale face shook. He wasn't ready to give in. He said, I was going to go to the ballgame, today, Henry. I had two tickets behind home plate.

I didn't know that.

Oh—*you* didn't know that. No shit.

I'm sorry.

Walbaum jabbed his finger into Henry's chest. He said, And do you realize you're tracking sawdust through my fucking house!

Henry stared at the floor. It was true. Oh god...I'm sorry.

I'm sorry. I'm sorry, Walbaum mimicked him.

You see, and that's from the bar, said Henry. There's evidence right there. Should I get a broom?

Shut up. No.

Henry stayed quiet for a moment. He felt sick. He was going to collapse. If everything was lost with Walbaum...if he couldn't win him back to his side...

As it were, Walbaum was screaming, Doesn't matter that we know each other our whole lives, when it comes to business, I'm a stubborn bastard. I have to be rigid in my practices. If I make exceptions for anyone it would disrupt the perception that people have of me. It might get out that *Walbaum* can be pushed around, that he caves in if you bitch and moan enough.

I'm sorry. I know, said Henry.

Oh *you* know.

No. No. I don't know.

Walbaum's crumbling nose wrinkled mad. He said, Home plate, Henry!

I'll buy you a new set of tickets.

You can't afford that. They were a lot of dough. And I know you don't have it.

Henry rubbed his temples. He badly needed water. It wasn't the moment to ask.

And today's a beautiful day to be at the ballpark, Walbaum screamed. You can't get *that* back for me. You *cannot* get *this* day back for me.

No. I can't, said Henry.

Walbaum's chest filled with air. What's happened to you. Two years ago, you were a different man. You had all this positive energy coming out of you. Now what do I see, you're sweating, and groveling—and to top it all off you got a real fucking button problem.

Henry snapped from his daze.

He said, *What?*

You heard me, Walbaum pointed at Henry's shirt. He said, You're missing all your fucking buttons. What's wrong with you!

Henry touched his chest. He said, Oh, right. They popped off in the bar. I was under a lot of strain. I'm telling you, these are just more facts to corroborate my story.

Walbaum let out a sort of caterwaul. Henry Schiller, he said.

Zachary.

Henry *ef-ing* Schiller.

What?

Walbaum didn't say more. All he did was dump the brown foamy liquid from the bottom of his cup into the sink and lay his hands down heavily on the kitchen counter.

Walbaum said, You owe me for standing me up today?

I know I do, said Henry.

That's good. That's a start.

Henry had a clear view straight back to the living room where there was a piano. Pointing towards the instrument, it was a Steinway & Sons, a grand piano, a beauty, Henry said, Can we get down to business?

Walbaum sighed. From one shoulder to the other he rolled his head. He said, You *owe* me?

I know.

You *do?*

Yes.

You *really* do?

Yes, insisted Henry.

All right. Okay. Let's go.

A moment later, Henry was seated at the piano. He could feel Walbaum's presence heavily over his shoulder, a dark figure. It was Paula who'd told him to always take a second during moments like these, those which could potentially make or break you, and think starkly about their importance. For most often the opposite was recommended. You were told to clear the mind. Empty it of thoughts. But Paula believed this was a mistake. She'd advised him to tell himself exactly what was on the line. Be bold. Fearless. You're meant to do *this*, to be right where you are. So lay out the consequences of failure. Be concise, and honest.

To himself, Henry said, Without Walbaum's support come tomorrow you'll be nothing but a lounge player with one testicle. You'll nail this, so help me god.

Henry began to play. He went easy into the intro, feeling loose. His shoulders were surprisingly relaxed. There was a slight tension in his neck, nothing more. His heart was open to the sound of the notes. It would be the song, he thought, that would define him. Listening to the first verse, he felt proud. What a relief. *Castrated New York* was a great song.

Unfortunately, like Paula, Walbaum seemed to think otherwise. Henry could sense him moving impatiently from one corner of the room to another. There was a bit of laughter from him, too. At the start of the last verse, he interrupted Henry.

Henry. Henry, he said. What are you playing for me here? Is this a joke?

Henry let up off the keys. He could feel beads of sweat rolling down his ribs. He said nothing.

Wasn't the first word of the song *impotent?* You can't start a song with that word. And all this mishmash of notes and dark, dark, dark everything. You're joking right? Play me the real song, for Christ's sake. The one for Bobby Jacques, yeah?

In his thumbs Henry could feel a strong pulse beating. He was going to lose his mind this minute. It was over. *This* was over. Walbaum didn't understand him, his art. Why did he ever think he would? Coming here in the first place proved he was a fool. He rested his hands in his lap, concealing his face. His stomach was wet with perspiration. What would happen to him? He'd end up *where?* In Riverside Park, maybe. Oh, he hated himself. He was an idiot, a moron. But it was obvious to Henry what he must do. He turned to Walbaum and placidly said, No. You're right, Zachary. That song wasn't for Bobby.

You had me worried there a minute, Walbaum chuckled. He patted Henry's back. That's good, though. Throw me a decoy. I like that. You're shrewd. So what's the song? You said the title was an acronym, some *C.N.Y.?*

No, Henry wagged his finger, utterly calm, as if there was nothing left to care for in the world. You misheard. I told you *M.S.…S.*

Well, whatever the fuck you said. Walbaum brought his sallow cheek next to Henry's. He said, What's it stand for?

Henry scratched his neck. He said, You're going to like this. It's called, *Miss Scandinavia.*

Walbaum scoffed. Real Cute. But Bobby's French. And she's a goddamn patriot!

Henry wasn't the least bit phased by this. He said, We'll call it *Ms. France*, if you like.

Ms. France? Walbaum fiercely shook his head. That has no ring to it, Henry. Do you hear a ring to *Ms. France*? Hmm?

Let me just play you the song, said Henry, his tone even, controlled. You're going to love it. I promise.

Fine. Play the fucking song.

Henry sat up straight, looked with earnestness at the keys and began. *Ms. Scandinavia* came in under three minutes. Lyrically, the verses repeated. After the second chorus came the bridge. A third chorus followed. During the outro, Henry sang again and again as the song would have it.

White nights,
White thighs,
Me and you,
Tonight.
White nights,
White thighs,
Me and You,
Tonight.
White nights,
White thighs,
Me and You,
Tonight.

When the song finished, Henry, pleased, even experiencing a kind of inner peace, turned to see Walbaum slowly walking up and down the room. Walbaum's eyes were closed. His lips were set firmly together. He stopped before a large window, and looked out through it, cracking his neck.

Well...well...well, he said.

Henry began to play Monk's *I Surrender, Dear.* He was gliding through it. He saw the end. Walbaum remained at the window, his back to Henry. He rose up onto his toes, his hands suspended on his waist. He turned to Henry. His expression was nasty. Henry quit playing.

I'll tell you what, said Walbaum...I will tell you *what.* Bobby Jacques, yeah, she's going to sing a song about Scandinavia whether she likes it or not.

Henry hadn't understood Walbaum. He asked him to repeat himself. But Walbaum screamed, Bottom line, she didn't sell two thousand copies of her last fucking record in Denmark and Sweden combined, and that's not going to cut it. Nope. *Uh-uh.* Play it again.

What?

I told you to play it again!

Henry, confused, started from the beginning. Between verses, he looked over his shoulder. There was Walbaum, listening from a crouched position. His fingers were splayed over his head. His lips were moving. When Henry finished, Walbaum told him to play it again. And again. Once Henry had gone through *Ms. Scandinavia* a fourth time, Walbaum began to explain how he already saw the video. It had many heaving breasts. Blondes were flowing from all directions.

With the song itself, which Walbaum called, A real hit, he said he might just sell a lot of records. He kissed Henry's brow. It was just what Bobby needed. Walbaum, becoming paler, and more frenzied, started going into detail about her last month in the recording studio. She was blowing twenty grand a week. But she hadn't produced a single song. She'd fired three engineers and four producers. The assistant to the original engineer, a quiet, Japanese boy whose name was lost on Walbaum, in addition to the musicians, who were an assemblage of her own personal entourage, all of them mediocre players at best, were the only persons she'd let in the door. She was wasting too many Brass Music dollars.

What I'm getting at, baby—and Walbaum had led Henry into his study and had a beer open for him—he'd even positioned a leather ottoman so that he could elevate his legs—is that you could really help Bobby?

How? What? I don't get it.

First off, said Walbaum, you could write for her.

Could I, though?

Walbaum slapped his hand to his head. What's wrong with you? You're a hit machine and you don't even know it.

No…I…don't…know it.

I need you over there helping her.

Over *where?*

Walbaum was too carried away by his own thoughts to answer. You'll talk sense into her, he said. You'll write songs together. Who knows, maybe by the end, you've written the whole record. That could be big for someone like yourself. And Bobby likes you. She thinks you understand her. Christ, no one understands her. She's not meant to be understood. That's part of her appeal.

Walbaum, hunched over his desk, shot out more and more information. He said, Anyway, the real question is when can I get you on a flight?

Henry stood from his chair. He didn't know what to do with his body, though, and he went straight back down into the chair again.

Could I have you there by tomorrow? Is there anything keeping you in New York? We'll buy your plane ticket, put you in a hotel, you know, two or three stars, no roaches, something decent. You'll be down the block from the studio. You'll straighten everything out with Bobby, get laid and forget your girlfriend ever existed. It's my most brilliant idea all week. But I need an answer, Henry. And I'd like it now.

I'm sorry. Where do you want me to go? Henry asked him.

However, Walbaum began pointing at Henry. His eyes were mean. He said, This wouldn't be a vacation. You're going there to work with Bobby. You'll get her in line. That's what I need. Once you say you'll do it, Henry, you're costing me money. *Not* that you'll have an expense account or anything fancy like that. No frills. Just a plane ticket, a hotel, and a chance to make some big songs. I could call Bobby this minute, tell her you're coming and that you're *her* man. What do you say?

What do I say to *what?* Henry cried.

And here, Walbaum came around his desk and grabbed Henry's face, tight in one hand. He said, What do you say to Paris, Henry! *Paris!*

EIGHT

Outside on the street, Henry hailed a taxi. When one pulled up he understood at once that he couldn't sit in a car and he told the driver he'd made a mistake, closed the door and began walking east. His mind was bounding forward. He required room, and full control over his direction. No, a taxi wasn't the place to put himself. He was grateful the thought had struck him before he'd shut himself inside the car.

He walked inside Central Park, and the next thing he knew he was calling Dahl. He got his service and left a message. Halfway to the East Side, on the path of the Reservoir and staring across the water at the space-bound rings of the Guggenheim, Dahl was calling back.

That was prompt, said Henry.

Henry, how are you? Tomorrow morning, eight o'clock, you'll be at the hospital.

About that, doctor, I have to ask you...The fingers of Henry's right hand hooked around the back of his neck. His nails dug there, into the skin. He said to him, If I were unable to make it...if I had to postpone the orchiectomy by a week, or two, or even three weeks, would that be possible, doctor?

Possible, Henry? Definitely not, he said. We have to get the testicle out of you. If we could have done it yesterday we would have.

And you're not exaggerating?

The question caught Dahl off guard. *Exaggerating*, Henry?

Because oftentimes doctors do that, for reasons of personal gain, and I just want to make sure you're being straight with me.

After a moment's silence, Dahl, maintaining his professionalism, assured Henry that he was being *straight* with him.

What kind of risk do I run putting it off a few weeks?

What kind of risk?

That's right, said Henry. What kind?

The doctor was speaking to him from out on the street. Henry could hear the squeal of car breaks and hard wind. Dahl didn't shout only to be heard above the noise, though. He was genuinely agitated. He said, Henry, if you don't come tomorrow, you might die.

Henry scoffed at the doctor. Cutting down from the Reservoir towards the Metropolitan Museum, evading a triathlon of bikers on the black road, he said, You're telling the truth?

Henry, I am telling you the truth.

Because you doctors...you take advantage of people like myself...people in weakened states.

Good god, Henry, please.

And we, the patients, we have no options but to take you at your word. I don't have any idea whether you're lying to me all this time. I'm not an expert. This growth, it could be nothing.

You don't believe that. I know you don't.

I'm not sure what to believe.

Dahl said Henry's name a dozen times, in succession. He told him, If you haven't understood me yet—and it seems you haven't—I'm telling you to *listen up*. The cancer is spreading through your body, Henry. It might still be contained in your testicle and all we'll have to do is get it out of you and have you seen once a month to have routine X-rays and blood work to make sure you're in good health for two years before you can go on with your life. If you wait three weeks I don't think there's a chance for that. The cancer will have almost certainly metastasized. It could go all the way into your brain.

My brain? said Henry, terror-stricken. Well...well, I'll probably be at the hospital tomorrow.

Henry

I said I'll be there. We'll get this testicle out of me.

Henry, said Dahl, his voice rising, I think you should come into my office in the morning and we'll talk. I'll meet you early. Six o'clock. We can go to the hospital together.

That's not necessary. I'll be at the hospital.

At *eight*? said the doctor.

At eight. No problem, said Henry. I have to go, doctor. Thank you. Goodbye.

He arrived home. Collapsing into bed he began to ask himself just why after being told by Dr. Glen Dahl, of Park Avenue and 74th Street, that he almost surely had cancer of the testicles, and receiving an ultrasound which confirmed the same, just why hadn't he gotten another opinion. It would have been the wise thing to do. But from whom would he have received this *opinion?* Yet another doctor. That was the real problem. He had no *real* options. It was go to a doctor, or die. That was how they sold it to you. They locked you down—your payment, thought Henry—by inciting fear. They were good at their business. Very good. He should only be so skillful with the sale of his music, he'd be rich. How much would Dahl receive from these efforts? And Munson? And Martz? And the hospital? And tomorrow's surgeon? And the oncologist who came after? And the pharmaceutical companies who manufactured his pain medicine? What was the grand sum of it all? He went to his computer and pulled up figures. He found that a man, Tom Hayman, who had had testicular cancer, and, without insurance he'd had to pay out of pocket:

Orchiectomy: $9,081.32
Initial urologist appointment: $213.00
Urologist surgical expense: $1,150.00
Hospital pre-operative testing: $522.00
Hospital surgical expense: $6,491.32
Anesthesia: $610.00
Urologist check-up one month after surgery: $60.00
Diagnostic testing: $24,999.80

Testicular ultrasound: $701.80
Pathology: $410.00
First CT scan (pelvis, abdomen, chest): $4,392.00
Second CT scan (head): $2,300.00
PET scan: $5,099.00
Third CT scan (post-chemo): $5,298.00
PET scan (post-chemo): $5,099.00
Pulmonary Function Test: $604.00
Initial PCP Exam: $120.50
Consultation with Radiation Therapist: $140.00
Medical Oncologist: $6,600.00
Chemotherapy Infusion: $32,270.00
Sperm Banking: $1,980.00

Sure they wanted Henry on the operating table. That was where the money was, their wealth, their families' futures, the children at college, the apartment in the city, and the second homes in the country. Nothing would be gained by telling him he was healthy and sending him out the door. So they started talking death. You might die. You will die. You're dying. Do you want to live? or to be phased out? Not to mention the pain. Can you bear the pain that'll come with ignoring our will? Do you know what real pain is? The pains of cancer? It looks like blood pouring from your mouth, like organ failure, like death. So you'll pay us. You'll pay because you want to live. And how else do you plan to do that? How else? Through prayer? Meditation? By ingesting exotic roots? Herbs? There's a reason humans live longer now, a reason you go on into your eighties, rather than perish at thirty—we, the doctors, keep you going. We're the ones. So, fork over your money and shut the fuck up.

Awful people, said Henry.

But he couldn't postpone the operation, could he? What if his illness worsened?

You might really die.

Maybe you've been bilked.

Have I?

I don't know, he said, to himself.

You could have the surgery in France. I hear they serve wine in the hospitals there. Sounds wonderful.

Could I really go off tomorrow?

He asked the question, aloud, staring out his window at the United Nations. He expected an answer to come.

Yet before one did, Paula called. It was just after six. She apologized for not contacting him sooner. She said she knew he was sorry for what he'd done, that he was upset with her for leaving for Europe, and so abruptly. She felt so guilty about everything. But tomorrow morning she was going away, and she had to see him. They must reconcile.

The dramatic quality of her voice, the passion, and urgency of it, made him feverish. He began to shake, with anger, and the irresistible desire to punish her caused him to break out in a sweat.

I'll pick you up at seven, Henry told her.

During the next hour, having left his apartment and begun walking back to the West Side, he thought, not of doctors, but of Paula's recital in Paris. More specifically, whether he might sabotage this most important occasion in her life.

How? First he'd get the address of Michel Drouot's home by telling Paula he must have it so he could send two dozen long-stem roses on the night of her recital as a token of his love and best wishes. On Saturday, he'd show at Drouot's in the early evening, however, wait outside till exactly the right moment, and come busting into the room mid-performance and make a scene. Pull hair. Spill drinks. Push the violinist from her chair. Or, beforehand, he'd find out where she kept her instrument and steal it. Who knew. There were so many possibilities. But he would not be swayed by her contrition, her kindness, or whatever love she might afford him this evening. He must be on guard against those things. He thought what he was feeling in his heart was real delight. Finally, he would make her suffer the way he had. He was deserving of this, too, he told himself. For all he'd gone through with Moss, this would be his reward. He couldn't wait for the time to come. It was all he wanted.

Turning onto 7th Avenue, a feeling of hopelessness penetrated his body. Nothing is permanent, he said, with an eye on the park up ahead. Still, she deserves hell for what she's done to me. Someone's got to teach her a lesson. I'm the best man for the job. Even a feeling of destiny about it, what with Paula playing in Paris Saturday and Walbaum sending me there tomorrow, it's undeniable. I have to be at the recital. The Universe has willed it. Such a big…big moment for Paula, she doesn't even know how big. Something for the ages.

He came up on Paula's building, a four-story brownstone green with ivy. Stunning—except behind that handsome exterior was Paula's renovated apartment, the kind they charged more for after stripping away every beautiful detail and putting in cheap new fixtures made in China. In the kitchen fake-wood cabinet doors hung off their hinges. Half the floor tiles in the bathroom were cracked. The floors themselves had been replaced with cheap parquet. Henry, though growling inside, still considered these abominations to the apartment's original design from downstairs on the street, waiting for Paula to step out. Minutes later, she did, wearing a narrow-cut blue dress. At the sight of her Henry's chest tightened. Then she kissed him on the lips, undoing the tension there. The temperature was warm, the air damp. On Columbus Avenue people dined on the sidewalks. Henry and Paula watched them feast, strolling along without speaking. To Henry, though, the silence was intolerable, and he pulled Paula to the curb. Staring in her eyes, he held her tightly at the wrist, not saying a word. He despised her.

I'm sorry I have to leave, Henry.

His gaze lowered in such a way that he could see his own nose. He pinched the tip of it and said, I believe you.

He hadn't meant to speak so softly, and with so much compassion. The anger in his breast should have made him choke on his words and cough them up when they were wet with bile. Nevertheless, he understood why he'd spoken in such a manner: Paula seemed especially vulnerable tonight. There was a sensitivity to her which began in her soft brow and continued down through her whole being. He wouldn't be swayed from his ire.

No, Henry bristled. I can't be.

They continued far up the avenue. To stoke his fury, Henry asked her to discuss Michel Drouot. What was the extent of his influence? What could he do for her? Paula spoke for the next twenty minutes without pause. Monsieur Drouot was an extraordinarily powerful individual. If it were his will, he could make her career. On the other hand, should he decide to do that, she'd still have to maintain her edge, keep her teeth sharp, she told Henry. But she'd known about Drouot forever. Everyone was aware of his influence. He had a golden touch.

As she spoke, Henry envisioned his hands around Paula's throat. Eventually he had to change subjects, he was so mad he couldn't walk straight. Reaching for any topic at all, he said:

Will you go to Italy while you're over there?

I will, she told him.

He missed the rest of her answer, distracted by a mental image of Michel Drouot, whom he guessed to be very short and thin, with silver hair and gray ravenous eyes, tossing her onto a four-poster bed, and jumping in after her. He didn't catch up with Paula's speech until she was telling him:

Let's turn around.

What's that?

I'd like to go back.

They'd come too far uptown from her apartment. They returned down Broadway. Paula began to apologize to Henry for disliking his song. I know you feel a lot of frustration. I try to be honest with you about your music. And *Castrated New York*...well—

I don't want to hear it.

Do you actually think that I'm such a horrible person, said Paula, that I'd want you to fail just to feel better about myself?

Did I tell you that?

In so many words.

Really!

Yes.

His heart was boiling with rage. Paula's wasn't. Why she was being so cool, he didn't know. He doubted she had so much patience in her heart. That wasn't possible from someone like herself. Her composure was an act, done to spite him.

I won't argue with you, she was saying. You can tell me anything you want. Her tone was brutally tranquil.

Anything?

Anything.

Do you mean it?

Why do you have to ask?

Henry, in the middle of the street, grabbed her by either shoulder. He looked her straight in the eye. He didn't believe he was going to say it. He hardly wanted to. But he did it. He said, I saw you with Jeffrey Moss on the boat in Central Park. You can't lie to me anymore. I know you're fucking him, Paula. I know it!

Or perhaps he'd only imagined himself saying it. Because, in meaning, Paula's expression didn't agree with this declaration. She was laughing. Her look was so full of good feeling.

She said, Do you mean it, Henry?

Do I *what?* His face was perspiring. He could hardly see. What had he said to her, anyway? He doubted that he knew. I'm sorry, I—*what?*

The light was changing. Traffic started towards them, and Paula led him up onto the sidewalk. She said, But do you really think you'd do it?

Really do *what*, Paula?

Do you think you'd visit me in Europe after your procedure?

I...but...are you sure that—

Her every part shone with affection for him. She said, I know it's expensive, but my parents gave me $25,000. I could pay for you to come. We could travel.

The wind, warm and smelling of the ocean, blew up the back of his shirt, and he caught the tail of it, stuffing it back into his pants. He said, Paula...I...I don't know what you mean.

I've always thought about us going around Europe together.

You have?

Yes, she said. You *knew* that.

And you'd be glad if I came to meet you?

So glad.

Really?

Take off work. Come.

Do you *want* that?

I'm telling you I do.

Are you really, though?

Why do you keep doubting me?

Is Jeffrey Moss not going with you to Europe?

I could pay for your whole trip, she told him. I would do it if it meant having you with me.

What are you *getting at?*

I want you to come meet me, Henry.

But he didn't understand. Was he not speaking the words he meant to say? Or was he saying them and she was refusing to hear them? He must be losing his mind. He must be. He must. He should tell her about his testicle. In an instant, everything would be different. Compassion would follow. But could he even utter the right words? And if he did, would she comprehend them? He tried again.

I have cancer of the testicles, he said.

And that's okay. You can come as soon as you feel better.

Ach, but why wouldn't she hear him? Was he saying something other than what he thought? Well, yes. That could be. Perhaps then he wasn't saying anything about Moss or cancer at all, but expressing his undying love for her. Or asking for her hand in matrimony. Though he thought he was standing, he might be down on one knee, proposing. Was that possible? Why not? Oh, he had to get out of here. He had to leave. To sleep. Rest would restore him. In the morning, he would go to the airport. He would fly to Paris. He would feel better there.

Everything's better in Paris, he told himself.

They were outside Paula's building. She said that staying the night was not a good idea. She hadn't even packed.

This is it, she told him.

Henry said, All right, and he began, by instinct, to kiss her. He used a lot of force. He remembered then how she preferred a tender kiss. He relaxed his lips. A moment passed, and he backed up a step and said, in a timorous voice, I'll see you soon, Paula.

You'll come to Europe?

I will.

Promise me.

Henry did promise her. He said, I'll come to see you. I mean it.

Her hand firm against his face, she said, *Please do.*

I will, he said. I promise, you'll see me soon.

Goodnight, Henry.

Goodnight. Goodnight. And he dashed off into a taxi.

NINE

Nothing can stop me now, thought Henry. He would travel to Paris to work with Bobby Jacques. He'd be present at the home of Michel Drouot Saturday for Paula's recital, as a saboteur, a lover, he didn't know which. His mind would not let him sort through an answer.

He lay down at a quarter after eleven to try and rest before a seven a.m. flight. Restricting his thoughts to the more mundane might bring on sleep, he knew. However, he couldn't stop fantasizing about Paula, Moss, Dahl, Walbaum, Bobby Jacques and his testicle. At a quarter to four he was still awake and staring viciously at the ceiling. Determined to leave for the airport in a half-hour, he went in the shower. Minutes later, under the rush of water, he noticed he was standing with palms up and feet splayed, the tip of his chin lowered to his chest and his eyes closed—he was nearly asleep. With a plane to catch, he slapped himself once, hard. From the shower, he began toweling off.

He saw his own white face in the reflection of the medicine cabinet, the dark circles, and the eyes themselves a bright red. His heart started to beat dangerously fast. He turned away. He had to get out of here. In the bedroom, he struggled into his navy suit and put on his black shoes. He locked the windows, shut the lights, snatched his bag and rushed downstairs onto the avenue. A dark sky covered the hushed streets of the U.N. Henry hailed a taxi. In the car and speeding through the jaundiced tube of the Midtown Tunnel, he had the feeling that his testicle had swelled to the size of an orange.

You're just deceiving yourself. You've always been good at that. Why do you fool yourself like this in the first place? What pleasure does it bring you? It is pleasure that you're after, isn't it?

Is it?

You want to imagine your testicle blown up, deformed, and to lose it...to absolutely lose it...

What pleasure do you receive in that? Pleasure should be sweet. And that's not sweet at all.

But you're so quick to assume that you're deceiving yourself. Perhaps you're not. You can feel the testicle big against your thigh. You can *feel* it. Can't you? Or are you imagining that, too?

Which is it?

Onto 495, with the Manhattan skyline turned down black behind him and his body snaked across the vinyl, he threw his hands down his pants, seizing his testicles.

What do you feel? If you say they're bigger, can you possibly be right? If you say they're just the same, can you possibly be wrong?

The question took a hundred shapes in his mind. Eventually the road bent right into the airport. The horizon was not yet visible. Planes were idle at the ends of jet-ways. The taxi pulled up outside the terminal, Henry paid the driver and went inside. His filter, the gray shading, was there, impeding his vision. The carpeted walls behind the checkout counter, the floors and ceiling, the television screens announcing arrivals and departures, all appeared dulled in tone. Checking in, Henry saw he had nearly two hours before his plane departed. Though most businesses in the terminal were still closed at this early hour, on the other side of security he saw a restaurant with its gates up and lights on. He went through the metal detector without setting off any alarms, and carried his bags into the restaurant. There was no one here. Henry plunged down in a chair. A tall and skinny redhead with a scar above his brow appeared seemingly from nowhere and dropped a menu on his table, heading towards the back of the room.

Can I order something? Henry called to him.

No, you *can't*, answered the waiter.

Why not?

'Cause the kitchen's closed for fifteen more minutes.

You have coffee?

I will, he said, once I've made some, and he went off briskly through a swinging door.

Fucking idiot, muttered Henry. Vigorously, he scratched the palms of his hands. He thought his forehead must be hot. He felt it with the back of his hand. And it was, yes. He must have a fever. But what of these televisions? All of them on mute. And there was one…two…three…four…five…six… fourteen of them showing the same local news channel. Why in god's name were so many televisions necessary? What was wrong with these people? Did they think this was a credit to their establishment? Did they think people wanted so many televisions? Disgraceful.

Henry, with commotion in his heart, took the menu in his hand and began to read the items quietly aloud.

A bagel and butter and a cup of coffee, was what he eventually told the waiter.

The waiter said, That's all you're eating?

That's all, said Henry.

No eggs?

No.

Juice?

Uh-uh.

Suit yourself.

I will, you prick, said Henry, to himself. This waiter and his *attitude*. What was his problem, anyway? Didn't I treat him politely, even after he was rude to me? Didn't I maintain a gracious look? I did nothing wrong. Nothing.

Here, the waiter, wearing a blue tie which matched his bright eyes, put a cup of coffee in front of Henry. The cup was filled only halfway. Henry, still the only patron in the dining room, pushed the cup to the side. He said to him, I'll take more coffee, please.

The waiter stopped short before rushing off into the kitchen, and shot Henry a hard look. Henry pointed in his cup. He said, You didn't fill it all the way.

Drink what I gave you, the waiter told him, then you can have more.

I know I'll want more, said Henry, so why not give it to me now?

You'll drink what I gave you first.

He was not a big man, the waiter. His arms were thin. His shoulders and neck were narrow. Henry, sizing him up, felt certain he could take him in a fight. But he dragged the coffee cup back towards himself, and said:

Fine. Thanks

The waiter went off. After a moment of consideration Henry began filling his cup with water. Drinking this mixture wasn't his intention. He gathered that the waiter, once returned, would think there was more coffee in his cup and he would wonder how Henry had come by it. Henry believed he suffered excessive pride. Because of this, he wouldn't ask how Henry's coffee cup levels had risen but let the question eat him up inside. Eventually he'd conclude that Henry had waited for him to go back into the kitchen, rushed over to the coffee machine himself and refilled his cup before he could be caught in the act. Of this, Henry was sure. So much so that among the empty chairs, Henry laughed an hysterical laugh, imagining the waiter's red-face darken with fury. However, at the next second, observing his coffee cup,

Henry noted how there was still room to add more water. He did, and the vision of his cup filling higher inspired him so much that he didn't stop until the coffee was spilling over into the saucer. Henry, his body shivering, was experiencing so much joy, he couldn't wait to see the waiter's expression at the sight of his cup. It would be priceless.

The waiter burst through the double-doors of the kitchen, and Henry's heart began to beat hard. The tense, thin redhead was coming straight towards him. Henry sat up eagerly in his chair, his smile crooked. Without acknowledging the overflowing cup, the waiter dropped a plate down in front of Henry.

There you go, he said.

The waiter went to stand at the bar. With the clicker up in the air above his head, he changed the channel on the televisions, the networks flipping at the same time on every box from local news to cable news to sports highlights to a cooking program, and finally more news.

But Henry couldn't believe what he was looking at. Before him on the plate was a bagel, black and smoldering. He pinched the edge of the table, letting out a cry. What was this? And what did the waiter mean by putting it on his table? There was no reason to ask. Henry knew quite well. He was trying to insult him. Did he think he'd get away with it? Did he? The answer was no. He would *not* get away with anything. Henry, flabbergasted, pushed back in his chair. The waiter was going around the room, putting salt and pepper shakers on tables. When he got to Henry, he stopped and said:

Is everything all right, sir?

No! shouted Henry, everything is not all right. You gave me a burnt bagel. You think that's funny?

Excuse me?

You heard me.

My, my. I guess I did, he said to Henry, stoic-faced. Must've not been paying attention when it popped from the toaster. Like me to put a new one in for you?

Oh, this waiter was crafty. A crafty, abhorrent man. But Henry could play his game…play it even better. Adjusting the crotch of his pants so as to avoid any disruption to his groin, he came from his chair. Biliously, he said, Perhaps I should go back there and do it myself.

What's that?

I said perhaps *I* should go back there and do it myself! I think that maybe…just maybe…you're a little fucking incompetent. Henry's eyes were riveted on the waiter, who had a thunderous look on his face.

Yeah…yeah, yeah, yeah, the waiter was saying. Do it. Go back there. See what happens.

Slamming his hand to the table, Henry told him, Take this fucking bagel back and bring me a new one.

Or what! What'll you do!

Henry, seething white with fury, said, Or, I'll kill you.

You'll kill *me?*

Yes!

Okay, come on, let's go. I'm going to kick your ass!

The two men charged at one another, their bodies coming down hard on the floor. Rolled under a table, spitting, grunting, Henry fastened his hands around the man's throat. Their faces were purple, sweaty, and their teeth flashed white. But Henry could see he was killing him. The waiter's blue eyes were partially raised from their sockets, and his embattled last gasps were enough to terrify Henry. He let go, jumping to his feet. The waiter was convulsing face-down on the floor. Henry rabidly paced. He began to apologize. He didn't know how any of this had happened. He was in complete shock. But could he forgive him? implored Henry. This was purely an aberration, a low moment. To strangle another man, to come so close to squeezing all the life out of him, he took it back.

The waiter, still fighting for air, said, You're going to jail.

Jail?

You assaulted me.

You assaulted me, too.

Did not.

You did! You *did* assault me.

Staring up at Henry from the floor, the waiter said the government would flag his name. He'd be put on a no-fly list, perhaps banned from air-travel forever. Whether there was any truth to this, Henry didn't know. However, taking his bag onto his shoulder, his body and mind daunted by these threats, he ran off. Was the waiter coming after him with a police officer at his side? He didn't look behind himself to find out, but went straight for the terminal exit. With no one on line at the taxi-stand, he got in the first car and told the driver to head into

Manhattan. His mind was in a state of turbulence. Are you mad? What if you'd killed him? *You*...a murderer. Facing a trial. Fifteen years. Twenty. Life. Those heavy shackles cutting into your wrists and ankles, that orange jumpsuit, your hanging head in the courtroom where your mother was present—everything would be different. Everything would be *over.*

Curled up on the backseat of the car, Henry wondered if he wasn't in fact running from the law. After all, he'd assaulted a man. (They'd assaulted each other.) But Henry had fled the scene of a crime. Surely an airport camera had captured his image. The waiter would identify him. They'd match his face to the names of passengers who'd checked in around that time. There couldn't have been many. The terminal had been so empty. There was no doubt the police would soon be knocking at his front door.

You're ruined.

The shivering of his body amounted to the first moments of a panic attack. He'd survived these in the past, the feeling that he was going into cardiac arrest, the pounding in his chest, the profuse sweating. The fainting. But he wouldn't be taken out by one of *those.* Impossible. He rolled down his window, the car speeding along the Van Wyck.

And yet he didn't trust himself. To think he'd nearly killed a human being. He could still feel the waiter's oily neck in his hands. He gripped the seat underneath him. You're mad. You're losing it.

A cold blooded...
You...you...you...,
Were seconds away from being,
A killer.
But that's not me.
It's not.
I'm under a lot of stress.
This is just what happens.
To go to Paris,
I should head to
Newark,
Airport.
They won't be onto me there I can buy a ticket and fly out,
Today.
That's the thing,
To do.

The panic in his nerves increased with this last thought, and he clamped his head between his hands, singing:

But you can't go to Paris,
You can't.
You need help!
There,
You said it.
I said it.
I need help
You do.
Can you get yourself

Into a psych ward?
Oh, god, if only…if only.
Just the thing to do.
But what if they say I'm crazy,
Then…then…then,
I'll be thought of as exactly that,
CRAZY.
For the rest of my life,
With the red stamp applied to the forehead,
The one that warns everyone,
That you're mentally ill.
Being hit with a lunatic stamp,
I couldn't bear it,
If people thought me…
Just under a lot of strain.
But there must be another way,
To check out for a while.
Some other way to get rest, maybe.
You could go to your mother,
Or, your father.
No.
Wrong.
Impossible.
Can't.
Some place must exist, though.
There must be somewhere that you can go.

And with the midtown skyline coming back into view, a solution came to mind.

TEN

Mr. Schiller, you'll feel a slight pricking sensation and when you wake, it'll all be over, said a woman's voice.

Henry, looking up from a table under the bright operating light, said, Thank you.

The prick followed, and he was out.

ELEVEN

When Henry woke, it was afternoon. He lay nauseous with his head raised on a pillow in a hospital bed, his abdomen in pain to the extreme, his testicle gone. His thirst was desperate. A nurse helped him to drink water from a plastic cup. Drowsy from the anesthetic, he fell asleep, till a doctor was there, describing the success of his surgery. To Henry, he looked to be only a hovering white coat, nothing more. However, his words were comprehensible. The testicle had been taken for biopsy. Pathology reports would come in a week's time and determine whether the cancer was benign or malignant, seminoma or non-seminoma, if there were any cancerous tumors in the lymph vessels, the seminal ducts, the epididymis or blood vessels, that is, whether the cancer had spread outside the testicle. If Henry were feeling up to it, he could have his CT-scans administered now. They would show whether spreading had occurred. The doctor would be looking in the retroperitoneum, he said, for enlarged lymph nodes, which, if discovered would indicate no less than a Stage II cancer.

Good, mumbled Henry. CT-scans. Let's.

Moments later, he was drinking barium sulfate with its hints of vanilla, butterscotch, and poison. The concoction allowed his organs and inner structures to be seen for observation. Once he'd had two servings, he would wait thirty minutes, then be taken over to radiology.

It was during his second glass of the stuff that Henry received a visitor. Orion Doherty, his bartender. Henry's vision had improved. He could see Orion's beard was closely shaven and his long, tangled hair trimmed short. But his black prescription sunglasses were the same. And, with the big belly, he still looked like Pavarotti or Francis Ford Coppola. What was he doing here?

You called me this morning, he told him, keeping a distance of several feet from the bed.

Did I?

What happened to you, Henry?

Unhesitating, he said, I had a testicle removed.

You what?

I have testicular cancer. They took out my testicle. Don't worry. I'm fine. He raised his cup of barium sulfate, as if to toast. The drink was already showing its effects. A warm current was passing through his body. He said, It was kind of you to come and see me.

You didn't give me a chance to say no, said Orion, quite seriously. When you called, I was in bed. It was six o'clock and I'd just closed the bar. You were raving. You said you'd almost killed a man and that the police might be after you, so you were going into the hospital to have surgery. I didn't know what you were talking about. You said I had to pick you up or else they wouldn't let you leave here. You were crying into the phone. What was I to say?

The story alarmed Henry. He said, You're sure that's what happened?

Orion told him, I'm sure. Who did you almost kill, Henry?

A waiter at JFK. We had an argument. I nearly strangled him to death. Then I came here.

Where were you flying?

Paris. I had things to take care of there.

Orion gave Henry's cheek a warm pat. His hand was the rough hand of a bartender. He said, You can tell me about it later.

The nurse assisted Henry into a chair and wheeled him to another room where a large machine, a CT-scanner, stood. More barium sulfate was administered, this time intravenously. On his back, and sliding into the scanner, like entering the eye of a Cyclops, Henry asked why he felt like he was urinating on himself.

A side-effect of the barium sulfate, said the woman administering the CT-scans. It'll pass.

Henry found that unbelievable. But changing the subject, he acknowledged how even John Glenn would feel claustrophobic in one of these machines. His comment was met with a feminine giggle, which briefly relieved him of discomfort. Next came the shrill, violent sound of the machine, like a jet throwing on its engines. And another, like a hammer coming down on a pipe: *Bang bang bang bang bang.*

Henry closed his eyes, and to himself, sang:

Bang.
Bang.
Bang.
Bang.
Bah-doo, bop-pop.

Orion took him home. He went to the pharmacy to get Henry's pain medication and stopped at the grocery, buying soup and yogurt, apple sauce, soft foods, as the doctor had recommended. He didn't leave the apartment, not even after Henry fell asleep, but stayed on the sofa. Henry, using the bathroom in the middle of the night, found him sleeping there. He was happy to see Orion. Getting to the bathroom on his own wasn't easy. The pain in his abdomen was severe. He had to support himself against the wall, taking small steps, one at a time. His apartment had an unfamiliar feeling, an emptiness which he attributed to Paula being gone from the country. At the toilet he decided to peel back the bandages covering his groin. Shaven bare, the skin black, blue and purple, at the sight of it he let out a gasp. His most precious area had been treated to the beating of its life. Like the eyes of the boxer following a match, it was monstrous. He felt he could sob for his testicle, gone from his body, in a lab and being picked apart, and in its place a prosthetic where he could not yet touch, the area too sensitive. He wondered how it would be to squeeze the prosthetic and feel no sensation there at all. The thought sent a ripple of despair through his body. Orion was asleep on the sofa. Henry shook him awake. Perplexed, in all his clothes, Orion leaned up.

Henry was saying to him, Please, stay for breakfast, would you? Don't leave so fast in the morning. Stay with me.

Okay, Henry. Okay. I will.

Thank you, Orion.

In the morning, Orion brought yogurt and coffee to Henry in bed. He was in too much pain to stand. His appetite was none. And now Orion was grating on his nerves. Henry couldn't stand to be taken care of. He didn't need help. He wasn't a child, but a grown man and could do for himself. Orion made it impossible to say any of this. To think, he'd offered to remain here for as long as he needed him.

Dahl called after eleven. He was glad Henry had decided to go through with the surgery. He had the results of his CT-scans. Great news. There were no enlargement of lymph nodes. The cancer had not spread to his abdomen, nor his pelvis. They still had to wait for the pathology report to come in, but the cancer was caught early.

How about that, Henry.

The doctor, having saved Henry's life, was clearly looking for him to share in his satisfaction. But Henry said, Doctor, I'm miserable. The pain is absolutely terrible.

I'm sure it is.

Henry, without saying another word, handed the phone to Orion. He said, Ask him if he has anything else to say, would you? and he closed eyes and fell asleep.

When he woke again he saw Orion in a chair, in the corner, reading through his songbook. Realizing Henry was awake, the bartender closed the book and placed it behind himself on a dresser.

Castrated New York. A good song, Henry.

Henry, evading the topic, said, I'm supposed to be in Paris. A friend over at Brass Records...well, he's not really a friend...we go back a ways, is the thing...Anyway, he gave me a job there. I should probably call him. I'm sure he's furious I didn't show up to work today.

Would you like me to call for you?

Henry laughed, and doing so strained his abdominal muscles. Wincing, he said, No. Thank you.

I can explain everything to him.

The man's a beast.

How bad could he be?

Henry shrugged. Sitting up in bed, he began tapping against his chin with the end of his forefinger. He said, If you were to call him, you couldn't let him know that I've been sick. You'd have to lie. Otherwise he might form a low opinion of me. I'll explain later. The point is that I *need* Walbaum.

You *need* him?

To have a career, to make money, to be someone—I need him.

Orion angled his head to one side and told Henry, I thought near-death experiences brought that kind of thing into perspective.

Henry said, No. They don't.

Why exactly do you have to lie to him?

Sighing from aggravation, Henry spoke of Walbaum's philosophy of putting money on the ill. He doesn't do it. And I don't like to let people know about my health, anyway. So if you were going to call him, you'd have to lie. Could you do that?

For you I would, Henry. I could say you were hit by a car.

No. Too much. How about, my mother's ill? Zachary wouldn't argue with that.

So I should make the call?

Fine.

Henry read Walbaum's number aloud from his cell phone, while Orion dialed. A look of great discomfort formed on Henry's face. To watch Orion speak of him with Walbaum, to overhear the discussion of his mother's health, his own absence from Paris, his future, would be too much for him to stomach. One of them should leave the room. It couldn't be Henry. He didn't have the strength. He told Orion to leave.

Get out of the room. Please, Henry was saying.

Orion was already on with Walbaum's assistant, though, and, at the next moment, with Walbaum. In the doorway, with his hand set on his waist, Orion identified himself. He said he was calling on behalf of Henry Schiller, that Henry's mother was ill, and for that reason Henry hadn't made it to Paris. He'd spent yesterday in the hospital. His mother wouldn't be fully recovered for some time. Her condition was a serious one.

That's enough, Henry told him. You don't have to let on anymore.

Orion, holding up a finger in protest, said Henry would contact him within a few weeks, once his mother was better. For a while afterwards Orion did the listening, with the phone held to his ear. His left arm rested across his sternum. There was something unnerving to Henry about its position. He didn't understand why any of this was taking so long. What could Walbaum possibly be telling Orion? What important information did he have to relay? The tension was stifling. He should have never let Orion call. He should have sent an email. But perhaps an email was too informal. Backing out required a phone call, even one placed by a person other than himself.

Now Orion lowered the phone to his chest. His eyes and mouth expanding with urgency, he said, Henry, the guy wants to know what your mother has.

What she has?

Her illness, said Orion, fervently.

Tell him it's a parasite.

Orion nodded his head in agreement. Into the phone, he said that Henry's mother had a rare parasite. Yet Henry had never said anything about the parasite being rare. Who'd said anything about *that?* Not Henry. Once Orion was off with Walbaum, Henry, lying flat on his back, let him know that he'd made an egregious error. The word *rare* had made it all seem like a lie. Any idiot could hear mendacity in *rare parasite* compared with plain old *parasite.* Orion denied that this was true. Besides, he told him, Walbaum wasn't upset by Henry's mother's illness and the delay it was presumed to have had on his departure for Paris. If anything, he was concerned.

Sure, said Henry. What you don't realize is that the man sets traps for people. You...you stepped right in one. Don't you see? He plays you one way and another so you think you're safe. Then he...he...

Henry fell back into his pillow. Orion watched him lose power, grief filling his eyes. He said it was time for him to go open the bar. If there were an emergency Henry could call him. Otherwise, he would talk to him soon.

Henry didn't expect Orion to leave so quickly. But he did. Well, anyway, Henry couldn't worry about the hurt feelings of another man. Not now. As for Walbaum, the relationship was all but ruined—*over*—on the mention of a *rare parasite.*

Bastards, every one of them.

To put an end to these thoughts, he took two pain-killers and went to sleep. For sixteen hours he lay unconscious.

And from vivid dreams interminably long to the sleeper, Henry opened his eyes. It was morning. He came slowly with teeth-gritting discomfort from his bed to the bathroom. The stool-softeners, recommended to him by Dahl, weren't helping. On the toilet a desperate pain assailed him. He couldn't push. Couldn't engage the abdominal muscles. But if he hoped to complete this evacuation, he had to do just that.

Owww, god. No, I can't. I can't. Maybe later.

Standing from the toilet, lifting his red pajama bottoms, he considered a shower. What he wanted more than anything, though, was to speak with Paula.

I miss her so much. I have to tell her I've been ill. She has to know. I should email her.

His computer bathing him in white light, on the bed, he began. He wrote pages about his health, and on his own future. Their future. He told her he would marry her. And mentioned his willingness to follow her anywhere. To become anything, professionally. He would get a *real* job was what he meant, and support her financially. Support her in all ways there were to support a person. He would change. Be better than he was. Accepting his limitations, he would set goals which were within his reach. Seek a more positive outlook. Think less about his own needs. Serve others. Relax.

He started over, erasing all that he'd written. His eyes glistening with tears, he smiled, rereading a passage about how much he believed in her talents. He removed those pages referring to Moss. Too negative. Assuring her that he would fly to Europe before long, he included an itinerary of their travels. They had to get to Ghent, but shouldn't only focus on the western half of the continent. What about the Ukraine? And he would like to see Romania.

Hours passed, and he didn't break from his writing. Then looking over all he'd said, he became suspicious. Caught up in a good time in a distant land, he reckoned the mind forgot what was left behind at home and shuddered at the thought of being dragged back to it against its will. Saying so much was the wrong thing. Wasn't it?

Be simple. Don't tell her much. Just the important parts. Or, maybe you're better off speaking on the phone. That way you can make sure everything said is understood. So then tell her you must talk on the phone. She has to call you.

Feeling this was the right choice, and with his head lifting before the computer, he typed:

Dear Paula,

I miss you. Please call me. Love, Henry.

And he hit *send*.

TWELVE

Word didn't come from Paula, not a call, nor email, or handwritten post. Henry treated his despair with painkillers, sleeping for sometimes twenty hours straight. He got up to use the bathroom and to drink water. He didn't eat. But first things first, each time, when his eyes opened, he checked to see if she'd tried to contact him. He'd find nothing. He called her father, careful not to sound as if he were after details which he himself could not attain from Paula with ease. Marcel appeared glad to hear from Henry.

Can you believe the success she's having over there?

With her recitals, you mean?

That's it, he told Henry. In Berlin, Vienna, Paris, she was the toast of the town.

Bitch, said Henry, to himself. And to Marcel, It certainly is amazing. Would you believe it, there's been good progress with *Miss Scandinavia?*

The company realized they'd made a mistake and called you back? he asked.

No. Not that.

A demo had been sent by Walbaum to Bobby Jacques in Paris. Taken with the concept of a *Ms. Scandinavia*, she'd recorded a cover of the track for her new record.

Good for you, son.

Henry thanked him. But at once, he felt embarrassed for having spoken to Marcel about *Ms. Scandinavia*. Really, what did he have to prove to the chemist? His daughter was no longer his.

The pain of romantic calamity overshadowed the significance of his pathology report. At the oncologist's office on East 68th Street days later, Doctor Voges, an elderly man, with hooded eyelids, a protruding stomach, and liver-spotted hands which pressed a clipboard to his chest, brought his patient through the results. As previously thought, Henry had testicular cancer. But the cancer had been contained in his scrotum. Unless he preferred to diminish the likelihood of a reoccurrence by some few percentage points, Henry would not have to undergo radiation treatment. X-rays and blood work would serve his purpose fine. They could begin next month, following up every month for two years. After which, Henry should be cleared to go on without further observation.

Henry, in a medical office, like any other he'd visited on the doctor-go-round, bright, with an antiseptic odor, the white linoleum floor tiles speckled black, blue and red, the doors metal and the air cold, was only half-paying attention. He couldn't consider his own health. Murderous thoughts about Paula consumed him. He had written again, but had heard nothing from her. He didn't understand. Why had she cut him off? The question ravaged him.

On his first night back at the Beekman, lofted over midtown, in a cool blue evening, old regulars filled the room. Where had Henry been? they asked. On vacation? Where to? He said he couldn't explain his absence. He excused himself, saying:

My break is over.

He started up with *My Funny Valentine*. The lounge was more than half-full. Henry hadn't the faintest idea that he was botching the song. His eyes were looking out through the window at a group of skyscrapers whose highest floors caught light from the westward falling sun. To himself, he was saying, Move on. Move on. You must move on. To the next thing. Please. Forget her. Get on to the important part.

From the bar now came John Grover in a gray pinstriped suit. Henry hadn't seen him come in and so he couldn't estimate how many old-fashioneds the U.N. *rapporteur* had already imbibed. The two men hadn't been in the same room since Henry had put Grover on his back over a year and a half earlier. But a running-joke played among the employees, from Edgar, to the bartenders and dishwasher. Before Henry left at night, someone would call out:

I hear Grover's downstairs on the corner waiting for you. He's got that deranged look in his eyes. You want someone to walk you home?

No, Henry would respond. I think I can handle him myself.

But are you sure?

Yes. Positive.

Grover came to lean on the piano, taking the pose which was once common for him here, with his frail but durable upper-body propped up on bent elbows. He stared at Henry with his lips drawn back and his gray, wasting teeth exposed. For a while, in the Deco lounge, he neither said or did anything. Henry, finished with *My Funny Valentine*, decided to come at Grover with Basie's *One O'Clock Jump*. The song's great rhythm and feel would disarm the ill-tempered man. But Grover didn't relent. Not even after Henry played *Honeysuckle Rose*, with its light and skipping humor, Grover moved only to drink from his glass. Sometimes his lips did form a scowl. Nothing more.

Until finally, Grover placed his glass on the piano. His dour face lurked above the highest of the treble keys. He said, You got a problem?

Henry, as if to sum up his defense, said, I'm just the piano player.

He's *just* the piano player. The old man's mouth narrowed with contempt. He said, If that's *true*, why is it every time I look at you, I want to give you a good sock in the face? Huh?

Henry could feel the swift beating of his heart. His hands were cool and sweating. Do not engage, he told himself.

I see my answer's right there in that look, said Grover. Yeah, whenever I see it—and that's every time I see *you*—I get the *urge*.

Henry said nothing.

Smug bullshit, said Grover. Pussy smartass. Come on. Don't think you can take on an old-timer like myself, eh?

I'm not going to fight you.

You're not, are you?

No, said Henry, still going on the piano, even smiling for the small audience gathered in the room.

Don't bullshit me. Outside. Come on. You and me.

But now Edgar Diaz came from his office. When he saw Grover, he quickly took him by the arm and led him to the elevator. He said he was no longer welcome here. However, Grover's ban from the Beckman didn't stop the employees' jokes from coming at the end of each night:

Yep, that's right, I hear Grover's outside on First Avenue for two hours. He looks angry, Henry. Well, don't worry, we'll get someone to walk you home.

THIRTEEN

Night after night in his apartment, Henry did battle his sinking heart at the piano. But he would transform his pain into music. He had no choice. He went to J. Van Gundy's and used the piano there. Orion, the man with the bourbon-wet mustache, and the two from the neighboring villages in Italy, could tell by the hostile look of him that he hadn't come to socialize, and they let him work on his songs undisturbed. (He had many new ones.) He was home by dawn, and slept till noon. His days were spent looking for Marshall Fleming. He often had nightmares about that poor man, ones in which he saw Fleming starving in doorways or being robbed of his last dollars by a band of kids from inside an empty train car in the small hours of the night, and another in which a horse, pulling tourists in a carriage through Central Park, trampled Fleming underfoot. After this last dream, he considered ringing Fleming at his apartment. He got all the way to his street. But fearful, he retreated.

Still, he checked for Fleming in Riverside Park. He went there today. A storm was hitting New York. Henry didn't own boots, and water came through holes in his black shoes making his feet wet. Trees swung mad in the wind. On none of the benches did he see Fleming. He stopped in at the tavern on Amsterdam. He wasn't here, either. But Henry thought he'd take a seat at the bar and have a beer until the rain passed. Maybe Fleming would show between now and then. He did hope so.

The tavern was filthy, and for that reason kept dark. Pink insulation hung down through crevices in the ceiling. It smelled of grease. Five rain-soaked men just off a night-shift sat quietly at the bar. Henry kept checking the door for Fleming. He prayed he'd come in looking clean and rested. For some reason Henry had linked his own welfare to this outcome.

Raising his pint glass to his mouth, he looked up, the sound of the bathroom door snapping closed had caught his attention. He saw a woman step from the back of the room. A phone behind the bar was ringing, and the woman, whose every move Henry watched with great intrigue, signaled for the bartender to answer. This clearly irked the bartender. But he picked up. When it turned out the caller wasn't looking for this woman, she moaned in frustration. Which caused the bartender to shout:

I told you you can't take phone calls here.

Blah, blah, blah, she said. She turned to Henry, and without pausing, went, It's that my phone isn't working. I live just upstairs. She pointed towards the ceiling.

Henry noticed her hands showed more years than her face. She stood close to him, her tall healthy body leant on the bar, her left leg pumping up and down, in agitation. She was saying:

There was a time when to use any phone at all you *had* to come down to the bar. A time when there was one phone in the whole town and everyone shared it. And *now* what? You ask a bartender if you can use his phone…and…and… it's, We don't allow freeloaders, which is what he said to me. I've used his phone *twice*. So what? I happen to have *just* a landline, and it's broken, and it's about as much fun trying to get the telephone company over to your house to fix anything as it is to sit in a shit-hole like this, surrounded by so many winners.

She paused, drinking. Tell me your name.

It's Henry…Henry Schiller.

Henry Schiller, she repeated, giving her head a quick shake.

She was in her late thirties or early forties. She wasn't so attractive, but she was in good physical shape. She wore tight blue jeans tucked into a pair of leather boots and her chest was large. A long piece of white ribbon was tied into her blond hair, the satin of which was made thin by the kind of nervous rubbing that she was doing to it at present. Keeping her eyes on Henry, she said, I'm Mallory. And if your phone ever goes out, Henry, and you need to call someone, you can come over to my house. I mean that. You live in the neighborhood?

I don't, no.

Doesn't matter. You come over. I live upstairs. I'm not in-town all the time. I'm an actress. I travel for work. But if I'm in town and you need to use the phone, you just come. You can use my phone. While you're at it, drink a cup of coffee, have some tea. I'm not going to make you a martini—she drew her glass close to her mouth—but who knows, maybe I will. If I'm in the mood. And maybe you really need a martini and—

Maybe, said Henry.

Right. Maybe you *have to have* a martini. Her energy seemed to leave her all at once. She sat pensively with her head sunk between her strong tan shoulders. Looking straight ahead, she said, I've been drinking martinis, Henry. I've been *drinking*, so don't mind me.

Henry didn't mind her in the least.

My phone was working forty-eight hours ago, she told him. I hadn't pulled it out of the socket yet. But I get this call...a call, Henry—and it's from Charles. Charles and I, we've been in a relationship five years. We live here in New York, and over there—she pointed towards the shadowed entrance—in Los Angeles, where we do a lot of work. The *funny* thing about Charles's call, Henry, is that that morning, before leaving the apartment, he tells me I'll see him later. He said *that* and now he's calling from our home in Los Angeles. He's calling from Los Angeles because he's flown there that morning, instead of going to a business meeting, which is where he told me he was going when he left the house seven hours earlier. So, I say, What are you doing in Los Angeles, Charles? And what does he say? he says, I'm not coming home. Very calmly, like nothing's wrong...like nothing's happened. You know when people do that, Henry...when they know they've fucked up royally and they take that *everything's normal* voice? I'm not coming home, that's what he says. Because Mallory...I think it's over. *Think* it's *over*? I say. What do you mean? And he says, I mean, it's over. And I say to him, Do you want to tell me what you mean, Charles? I mean, really...tell me what you *mean*. And he says, If you want to know the truth...I'm disappointed in our sex life and...and...and I don't feel like...get this, Henry...you won't believe what he says, he says, I don't feel like a man because I'm not *free* to go around *fucking* as many women as I want. Okay? So that's what he tells me, Henry. And this was two days back when my phone still worked, before I'd ripped it out of the wall.

Henry watched her dark lips move and her long pale throat tense and un-tense while this speech poured from her. Her brow was knitted over light eyes, and her chin slightly trembling. A strand of her hair, long and blond and damp from the rain, was being twisted in her left hand next to her ear.

She said, Charles went up the West Coast six months ago to visit an old college friend who's been living in a sex-commune growing fruits and vegetables and fucking for hours every day for *six years*. And get this, Henry, at this mental ward they call a commune, they've got philosophies about *life* and how we're meant to live it, and living up to your *sexual potential* is one of their main tenets. They believe you have to be out there *fucking fucking fucking* all the time,

Henry, and that all mental and physical illness result from the sexual limitations men *and* women put on themselves by having just one partner.

Mallory explained to him how at the commune monogamy was believed to be the cause of cancer, heart disease, even schizophrenia. Because a man's *brain* always leads him to the next woman. But most men are telling themselves, *No,* I can't do that. I can't fuck her...I *cannot* fuck *her*...just this one here, my wife, my one and only, because these are the rules and I like my life enough not to break them. I have a home, a bed and comfort...And so my sex life begs for more, begs for change...*begs*...so what. So life isn't perfect. I don't need perfection. In other words he creates barriers in his head—*walls*, Henry, *walls*—doesn't let himself think about what he *really* wants...and what he *really* needs...and this process is devastating to men, they say, because they're built to want to fuck everything that moves.

Her hands came down flat on the bar, her tense fingers spread wide apart.

In the commune, she told him, one of the rules is that if you're walking along and feel like having sex, man *or* woman, you can ask someone to do it and they have to consent. Deny the privilege, you're kicked off the premises. That's the rule, Henry.

The rule?

It gets worse. Three sessions a day...*three*...every day, each one forty-minutes long, you and an assigned partner just go at it...you *fuck*, Henry, according to a schedule. Repulsive, right? I mean, just disgusting.

Yes, Henry said. That's—

And at night…the worst of all…they come together to discuss something they call *sexual blocking*. It's what I was describing before: the act of refusing oneself permission to have a thought or desire for reasons of guilt or disgust or fear. And these psychotics out West, they spend their time getting it all out, telling their tales, trying to cure themselves of internal wounds *incurred*, they say, in these moments of denial. Fucking creepy, isn't it? I mean, *fucking…creepy*. So, anyway, Charles wants to move into this commune. He's acting like it's a medical emergency…like he's dying and this is the only way he can save himself. I even said to him, I said, So what, you're dropping out? And he said, I'm getting help. *Help*? Help, Mallory. I have to take care of my body, and so do you. Maybe you want to consider visiting a place like this one day. Not this one, *per se*, because I'm here and it wouldn't be good for either of us to be together here. But another commune, someplace else. You could live in a community that helps you to truly fulfill your *sexual potential*. And this was when I pulled the phone out of the fucking wall, Henry. I just yanked it out. And I haven't spoken to Charles since. I'm trying to get over him.

Henry watched her finish more than half her martini in one sip. But he was wrong to think alcohol was her sole means of forgetting. For, the next thing he knew, she was dragging him up to her apartment, biting and pulling at him, tearing at his clothes, in a dark hallway. She took her shirt over her head and pushed Henry's face into her large, supple breasts, and said, Like 'em, Henry? Do ya?

Oh, yes, he said. Yes!

She pushed him through a door which led into her apartment. Another shove sent him straight back into the bedroom, and onto her bed. With her hands behind Henry's neck, she pushed his face down into her stomach and said, Take off my pants and fuck me.

However, she didn't give him the chance to remove her clothes, but started pulling on Henry's belt-buckle, undid it and slipped him out of his pants. Mallory, seemingly in a great hurry, said, I'm on the pill. You can go right in. She then put him inside her.

This full-bodied woman was now on top of him, moving to and fro. Henry feared for the place above his groin where he'd been stitched up. (This was purely mental. It had long since healed.). So he flipped her over onto her back. She seemed to like being taken so firmly around the waist. Going at it still, he began singing in his head:

You're making it.
You are making it.
You're making it.
You are making it.
You're making it.
You are making it.
You're making it.
You are making it.

Then he let these lyrics go, and lost himself in the act.

When they were finished, Mallory went to the bathroom. Henry saw that her room was in great disorder. There were clothes and half-filled water-glasses and newspapers and magazines everywhere. He stretched out on the bed, his mind still, his body tranquil. It occurred to him that he had seen a piano when entering the apartment. Hadn't he? He could have sworn he had. He put on underwear and went out of the bedroom. And there it was, a white standup piano wedged between over-stacked bookcases. Without sitting at the instrument, Henry's fingers came down on the keyboard. His right hand did a little trill. He played a verse of *Don't Fence Me In*. Before he knew it, though, the first chord of *Castrated New York* had rung out. He began to sing. In the middle of his playing, Mallory came from the bathroom. Naked, and with her blond hair tangled, her body fell heavily on the piano bench. In the slight movement of her shoulders was something flirtatious. Her eyes glimmered warmth. She asked him what it was she was hearing. He named the song. She made him play on, and on.

This is really good. You wrote it?

I did, he told her.

I'm impressed.

Are you? he said.

Very.

By nightfall, they were eating Italian on a side-street in the East 60s. Mallory couldn't get over his talents. She said he *had* something. Something undeniable.

But give me the chorus one more time.

He laughed, and began to sing for her.

They started dating. Henry told her he'd never been happier, a falsehood. Paula wasn't gone from his mind.

He couldn't help feeling the occasional burst of rage, or the kind of hot sting which makes you grab the edge of the bathroom sink and curl your toes to regain control when you're brushing your teeth at night. He couldn't believe that he had never heard from her. The same with Dr. Andrews. He thought there must be something about himself which made it impossible for these women to give him an explanation before ending communication. Something in his character. He would get to the bottom of it, perhaps in a song. From various people he came by different stories about Paula. One, that she'd never come home from Europe. Or that she'd started up a relationship with a wealthy South African businessman and moved to Johannesburg. Henry preferred to know nothing about her. He was sure she was fine wherever she was. Perhaps playing violin. Perhaps not. Virtuosos were notorious for burning out fast.

In fact, one evening he did come face to face with her.

Walbaum had been after Henry to write for the alumnus of one of last decade's network talent-shows, and he sent him down to a venue on West 26th to see the artist perform. Henry was so grateful to have Mallory with him. These scouting trips were pure torture. All the waiting around on one's feet. The drunk crowds. But Henry didn't know if she should be with him tonight, she'd been fighting a cold. The venue was hot, stuffy, unpleasant for a person who wasn't at her full-strength. She said she would make it, nevertheless. Besides, Henry had begged her to come with him and she wouldn't abandon him now.

Henry put his arm around her waist. Mallory—she wasn't as pretty as Penelope Andrews or anywhere near as talented as Paula. Colette Jacques was sexier. And yet Mallory had a larger chest, which went some ways in making other men jealous. Her eyes were free of bitterness. He looked into them now, feeling the moisture on his own face, and smiled at her. The singer performed a number of cover songs, all Motown. Certainly he had a great voice. Henry had been told by Walbaum to go shake his hand after the show. Mallory couldn't make it to the end. She was tired. He put her in a taxi, saying he wouldn't be far behind. The sidewalk outside the venue was crowded with men and women smoking. Henry did love the smell of tobacco. He wasn't in a hurry to go back in and watch the performance. He asked a teenager for a cigarette, and a light, then stood next door to the venue in front of a restaurant, smoking.

Here, the door to the restaurant swung open by force of a hand whose body could yet be seen by Henry. Though the person was shouting into her phone, it was the hand, not the voice, which made Henry look on, with fear. He knew it. The long, bulbous nails, the protruding blue veins, the white polish. She hadn't emerged through the door, not yet.

Tomorrow…tomorrow, the voice was saying. As early as 4:30 in the morning. I'll be awake.

Rain started coming down in a light mist, though not enough to force people back inside. Henry, perfectly still, continued looking at the hand. He didn't know if he should step around and see for sure that it was her. He'd been wrong many times in the past, thinking someone might be Paula on the street or getting out of a car. His heart would begin to race and he would become sweaty, nauseous. Luckily, that hadn't happened for a long time.

Now Paula brought her head through the doorway. Staring inquisitively at the brown sky, her small nose wrinkled, she seemed to be thinking through some piece of business. Her head turned, then, and she looked at Henry.

Is that you? she said. Her expression was all excitement, thrill.

Henry wasn't sure he could speak. His stomach felt wired tight to his throat. He let out a firm, Yes, it is *me*.

What are you doing here?

Where should I be?

Her smile widened. Exquisite in a black dress, she wore little makeup, only mascara, and no jewelry. Her short dark hair was slicked back. She hadn't lost any of her self-assurance. And her astonishment didn't quit.

I can't believe it's you...Henry Schiller, she said.

Using his last name in addition to the first made him seem unfamiliar. Yet Henry felt like the same person he had always been. And she knew him, and he knew her. So why pretend?

How are you? he asked.

I'm well. Very well.

Paula told him she'd been living in London, playing concerts throughout Europe. The wife of a shipping magnate had bought her a pied-a-terre near Lincoln Center to stay in when she was in New York. She was very happy there.

That's good, Paula.

And you, Henry, she said, how's everything going?

He explained that someone was performing next door tonight for whom Walbaum wanted him to write. It satisfied Paula to hear Walbaum's name, to have that special knowledge of Henry's life. Her blue eyes sharpened. Stuffing her cell phone back into her purse, she said:

I'm happy to hear you two are working together.

Henry, letting his cigarette fall to the street, wouldn't allow her to take this comfortable tone with him. He changed subjects, asking her about her father and stepmother. But Paula didn't want to talk about them. She politely explained then that she was making someone wait for her alone at a table. She began saying goodbye. Before she got away, Henry spoke the words:

You received my emails, didn't you?

What's that?

The emails I sent you, you got them?

The door to the restaurant swung open, choppy white noise washing over the street. Paula's head fell to one side. Something in her face, still not a woman's but a girl's, lit up at him. Henry couldn't believe his nervousness. A year and nine months had passed since he'd last seen her, he thought his feelings for her had been eviscerated by time. It was worse than ever, though.

Turning out one hand beside her slight body, her eyelids fluttering, she said, My focus has always been my career, Henry.

I *know*, Paula. I mean, I knew that.

And I was sure you were already seeing someone new by the time I was back in New York.

I was, he said, his spite apparent.

You see, I knew that.

She touched his shoulder, her fingers on his collarbone pressing gently for a moment. Henry's whole body awoke with terror. In his black shoes he leaned away from her, skittishly. He waited for the feeling of her touch to fade. When it did, he said:

I just don't understand why you didn't call from Europe. I had written, asking you to call.

Henry, she calmly stated his name, I picked up the phone a few times. I couldn't dial it.

Why not?

She didn't answer his question. What she said was, I didn't mean to hurt you.

The knuckles of her right hand were suddenly pressing on his chest. What a deranging power she kept in that hand, Henry could feel the life slipping in and out of him, his belly warm. He stared up at fast-moving clouds made visible at night by the bright city lights. The rain was falling harder. A taxi stopped at the curb and two couples ducked quickly inside the restaurant. Henry could see Paula's eyes follow after them. Any second now, she'd leave and go back to her table. He drew her by the elbow under a doorway, out of the rain.

What is it, Henry?

His hand left her elbow and went into his pocket. He said to her, Why did you disappear on me?

Frowning above crossed arms, she said, I was off working. I couldn't think about anyone else.

What about after?

There hasn't been an *after.*

For a few seconds he experienced intense jealousy. It was precisely her kind of attitude which was needed if you were going to do anything worthwhile in this life. She was the real thing, Paula, unapologetically focused, brutal, and talented. He would never rise so high, he knew. Neither would he let her think any part of him accepted these qualities in a person.

He said, I had plans for us. I wanted to marry you, Paula.

Henry—

I did.

I'm only twenty-three.

So.

Henry, I wasn't ready to settle down.

Will you ever be? 'Cause I don't think so, he said, not giving her the chance to answer him. You either have it in you always or never at all. That's the truth.

I don't agree.

Oh no?

At this time Paula told him she had to rejoin her friend in the restaurant. She said, We should get together when there's more time.

When will that be? he asked her. His forehead was tilted towards her, expectantly.

I'm busy all this week. Maybe next week.

Next week?

Yes.

Okay, Paula.

Call me.

I'll call you next week.

She kissed him on the cheek, then went quickly away.

Henry returned next door to the venue. However, backstage, and introducing himself to the singer, he was filled with regret. He should have asked Paula to meet him later for a drink. Next week something would come up in her schedule. She'd be invited to play some recital in Santa Barbara at the last minute. She wouldn't be able to see him. They would never have the chance to resolve their past. He should have acted immediately, when he knew where she was.

He hurried back to the restaurant, but Paula was gone. At once, Henry, with a searing pang in his chest, decided it was for the best that she wasn't there. He should never speak to her again. Never see her. If she called him next week, he would tell her that. Then it was decided.

That's it, he said, to himself.

He went home to Mallory. He found her asleep, in bed, and tiptoed into the kitchen, pouring himself a tall glass of red wine. He didn't know what to do next. For a while he stood at the window. A double-length bus came hard up the avenue. When it passed he could see nothing more moving below.

If she calls, he thought, you don't even answer. You do not answer.

He turned the television on, shutting it off right away. It wouldn't hold his attention, he felt sure. He opened a book on ancient Rome, then closed it. There was his piano. Mallory had bought him a narrow green vase, wide enough for only a few flowers. She had been replacing them before they died. Three yellow tulips, their petals open, leaned inside the vase at present. Henry sat down at the instrument. At first, with his hands on his lap and eyes closed, he did nothing. He was using the piano bench as a place to be. He had no intention of playing. Anyway, the hour was late, and Mallory was sleeping. But then at the next moment, his hands did lift, and they were suddenly on the keys. He struck one, quietly. It was a high up note. He followed with the key beside it, and now another, and one more.

It was a problem he'd had since as far back as he could remember, whenever he was at the piano, if he wasn't working in a club, say, or with an artist, he would try to write something new. That is, his mind would demand that he try and create a piece of music. What he wanted, though, was to be able to sit down at the piano, and just play, for the sake of amusement. There were worse problems to have. And still, he took his very seriously. One day he would like to be the kind of person who just let go. As it were, he now began to write a song (one which didn't take long to find and lose itself). The music was there, at his fingertips, ready to be played, (and then spilled off into nonsense). Same with the words, (here, gone). He sang:

From the moment,
They descended,
His fate,
Was,
Decided.
And what happened after,

BALLS

Was a twinned,
Command.
Up, down,
Walk, run,
Stop, strike,
March.
And when would,
He sleep?
He was in love,
And you made it,
Happen.
Before there were,
Cities,
There were,
Those two,
Committees.
Before there was…
Shh…
Shut up…
You must,
Call Walbaum tomorrow,
And let him know you loved,
The artist you saw tonight,
That you want to work with him.
You're broke,
In debt.
Edgar Diaz,
Tell him you want,
More nights,

At the Beekman.
It's almost time to pay
Your rent.
Impotent, I blame the powers,
That have without conscience,
Watered-down the streetscape,
(I.e. he who has erected a,
Residential tower fast and cheap,
So as to fill it up with new,
Paying residents.
But Walbaum's right,
You fool.
You can't start a song,
With the word,
Impotent.

Acknowledgements

The author would like to thank: Lisa Weinert, Tyson Cornell, Will Akers, Alison Klapthor, Alison Moran, Spoon, Vikash Shankar, Jacob Bauman, Norman Buckley, Stephen Daldry, Dominic DeJoseph, Josh Brown, Harvey Goldberg, and Jenna Gribbon.

Additional Material

Julian Tepper

The Paris Review Daily, December, 2012

"In Which Philip Roth Gave Me Life Advice"

Roughly two weeks ago in the dining room of a Jewish deli on the Upper West Side (whose name, for legal reasons, must remain undisclosed) I served Philip Roth his usual nova, eggs, and onions (egg whites only); a bialy (hold the cream cheese and butter); and a large, fresh-squeezed orange juice. He was once a more regular patron, but I hadn't seen Roth at the deli for nearly a year—he does reside in Connecticut—and during the last two months I'd been looking forward to his arrival with heightened anticipation. With my debut novel, *Balls,* now published, I would conquer my nerves and give him a copy. Sure, many months before I had heard him say in an interview that he no longer read fiction. But his reading the book was not the point: having worshiped at the Roth altar for more than half of my thirty-three years, it was simply something that had to be done. And here was my chance.

He was seated alone at a table, reading on an iPhone and awaiting his check. I approached Roth with less trepidation than I had anticipated, given that in past years, the author's presence had been enough to make me physically ill and render my hands so shaky that I would drop plates, spill coffee, trip on air. He looked ... well, he looked like Roth: ruddy skinned, dark eyes stoical, bushy eyebrows untamed, shoulders back in a noble posture. Against my boss's orders (I've actually signed a piece of paper that said I wouldn't write about patrons or bother them with things such as my novel, the consequence being my termination ... I hope I have a job tomorrow, the child will need diapers!) I keep copies of the novel in a knapsack under the waiter's station just for moments like these. I tucked one under my arm. With every table in the dining room occupied and me, the only waiter, neglecting the needs of a good fifty patrons, I approached Roth. Holding out *Balls* as a numbness set into the muscles of my face, I spoke. "Sir, I've heard you say that you don't read fiction anymore, but I've just had my first novel published and I'd like to give you a copy."

His eyes lifting from his iPhone, he took the book from my hands. He congratulated me. Then, staring at the cover, he said, "Great title. I'm surprised I didn't think of it myself."

These words worked on me like a hit of morphine. Like two hits. It felt as if I was no longer the occupant of my own body. The legs had gone weak, the ears warmed, the eyes watered, the heart rate increased rapidly. Barely able to keep myself upright, I told him, "Thank you."

Then Roth, who, the world would learn sixteen days later, was retiring from writing, said, in an even tone, with seeming sincerity, "Yeah, this is great. But I would quit while you're ahead. Really, it's an awful field. Just torture. Awful. You write and write, and you have to throw almost all of it away because it's not any good. I would say just stop now. You don't want to do this to yourself. That's my advice to you."

I managed, "It's too late, sir. There's no turning back. I'm in."

Nodding slowly, he said to me, "Well then, good luck."

After which I went back to work.

In the two weeks that followed our exchange, I've mentally replayed the moment again and again. And the conclusion I've most often drawn was that if I hadn't been drugged by his compliment, by his presence, by the fact that he was actually engaging me in a conversation about writing, I would have asked him not whether he would have traded in all the celebrity, the money, and the sex to have lived the more plain existence of, say, an insurance agent. No, I would have asked him about boredom. And though I have only one novel published—and experienced none of the success of Roth—I still feel strongly that the one thing a writer has above all else, the reward which is bigger than anything that may come to him after huge advances and Hollywood adaptations, is the weapon against boredom. The question of how to spend his time, what to do today, tomorrow, and during all the other pockets of time in-between when some doing is required: this is not applicable to the writer. For he can always lose himself in the act of writing and make time vanish. After which, he actually has something to show for his efforts. Not bad. Very good, in fact. Maybe too romantic a conceit, but this, I believed, was the great prize for being born ... an author. And in the two weeks leading up to Roth's announcement, this was what I mostly thought about when considering what I would have said if I had remained in my right mind while in his company.

And now Philip Roth has told us he will no longer write. I wonder, what will he do when boredom sets in?

Elizabeth Gilbert

Bookish, February 4, 2013

"Roth's Complaint: Elizabeth Gilbert Takes on Philip Roth"

Reader, our sincerest apologies. Due to licensing complications, we were unable to obtain the proper rights to reprint this essay. However, it is easily accessible online.

ROTH'S COMPLAINT

ROTH'S COMPLAINT

Julian Tepper

The Daily Beast, February 6th, 2013

"Leave Philip Roth Alone!"

Dear Philip Roth,

Look, I have to apologize. You told me to quit writing. It was a terrific moment in my life. I went and wrote an essay about it and now people are angry. Elizabeth Gilbert is angry. People listen to her. They love her. Now they're not happy with you. But then people are reading negativity into an incident where there was none. Having been there, and lived through it, and with the backlash, I wanted to write you and say I'm sorry. Since I don't have your address, I've chosen to reach you through the media. I hope you get this.

First, let me say that it was not the first time I had been given that same advice to quit writing. Though it's cliché to bring up one's grandparents when discussing the inspiration behind becoming this or doing that, because you and my grandfather remind me of each other and have both played some role in my becoming a writer, I must talk about him now. He lived and worked at his loft on West Broadway, and when I paid visits to him, he'd come out of his studio, though only for a brief time, for he had to get back to work, and usually right away he'd ask how the writing was going. Before I'd answered him, however, he would have already told me not to be an artist, that I was setting myself up for a miserable existence, and that, if indeed I had to do this, to at least ... at very least ... marry a wealthy woman. "Forget what you've read about the garrets and the gutters, there's nothing noble about poverty! If you have to write, make sure she's got bucks!" "But what about love!" To which he would respond, "Shut up!"

Next, my grandfather would ask me what time I was waking up each day. Anything after 4 a.m. was too late. I was being lazy. Yes, 4 a.m. was the time to get up. This was when an artist should be getting to work. Before the farmer. Before the world. 4 a.m.! "Do you want to make good art, or crap? "You get out of it what you put into it." "Use it or lose it." These were his lines, and in the few minutes that we would speak he'd use them on me, like he was Bobby Knight or Bill Parcells. He had a round, very wide face, light eyes full of pride, a dimpled chin, a bald pate with a gray fringe. Why bring up his features? Actually, they are relevant. Because after his words on being an artist, and before returning to his studio, he'd say to me, "I used to be the most handsome guy in any room. But God's great joke is to make us all look so ugly at the end. Well, anyway, Julian. That's it, I've got things to do."

Other advice from my grandfather: don't talk about your good luck; you'll live if you're lucky; get back to work; shut up.

Mr. Roth, my mother always used to say to me, "Know your audience." As far as our encounter went, it's fair to say that you knew yours. When it comes to writing, I am of your school. It's a brutal field, not warm at all, filled with disappointment. From where I'm standing, I wouldn't even say you were giving me advice. We were just talking about making art.

Again, I'm sorry if my piece has led to some bad press. (My grandfather never said anything about all press being good press, but he wasn't into the press, and I'd venture to say that you aren't either, so I want to try to put a positive spin here.) But clearly you were not comparing writing to all the very worst professions (lawyer, stockbroker, real estate developer, etc). And as far as my piece in *The Paris Review*, it had something to do with meeting a hero. It had less to do with one of the greatest authors of the last century's advice to a young novelist. And what I don't want missed here is its central point, born out of the announcement of your retirement, which addressed one of the reasons why to write at all if writing is, as you told me, "Just torture. Awful." To keep that point from being lost, I will quote from the essay that has led to this apology:

"In the two weeks that followed our exchange, I've mentally replayed the moment again and again. And the conclusion I've most often drawn was that if I hadn't been drugged...by the fact that he was actually engaging me in a conversation about writing, I would have asked him not whether he would have traded in all the celebrity, the money, and the sex to have lived the more plain existence of, say, an insurance agent. No, I would have asked him about boredom. And though I have only one novel published—and experienced none of the success of Roth—I still feel strongly that the one thing a writer has above all else, the reward which is bigger than anything that may come to him after huge advances and Hollywood adaptations, is the weapon against boredom. The question of how to spend his time, what to do today, tomorrow, and during all the other pockets of time in between when some doing is required: this is not applicable to the writer. For he can always lose himself in the act of writing and make time vanish. After which, he actually has something to show for his efforts. Not bad. Very good, in fact. Maybe too romantic a conceit, but this, I believed, was the great prize for being born … an author …

And now Philip Roth has told us he will no longer write. I wonder, what will he do when boredom sets in?"

One last time, I'm sorry.

Sincerely,
JT

David L. Ulin

Los Angeles Times, February 6th, 2013

"Writing is easy: Just open a vein"

Bookish is a joint venture of Hachette, Penguin and Simon & Schuster (three of the so-called Big Six publishers): part editorial and part e-commerce, not unlike Goodreads, although without the social media component. It launched on Monday evening and I have no idea whether it will be successful—although the fact that the site is offering original content is encouraging.

The Gilbert essay is the first such effort, a take on Philip Roth and his reaction to a young writer who pressed a book on him. That writer, whose name is Julian Tepper, blogged about the experience in late December for *The Paris Review.*

Tepper is a waiter at a Manhattan deli Roth frequents; he handed over a copy of his first novel, *Balls*, while Roth was eating "his usual nova, eggs, and onions (egg whites only); a bialy (hold the cream cheese and butter); and a large, fresh-squeezed orange juice."

Roth's reaction? He congratulated Tepper, then added, "with seeming sincerity": "Yeah, this is great. But I would quit while you're ahead. Really, it's an awful field. Just torture. Awful. You write and write, and you have to throw almost all of it away because it's not any good. I would say just stop now. You don't want to do this to yourself. That's my advice to you."

Gilbert uses this as a starting point to take on the idea of tortured writers in general and Roth's struggle in particular, asking, "[S]eriously—is writing really all that difficult? Yes, of course, it is; I know this personally—but is it that much more difficult than other things? Is it more difficult than working in a steel mill, or raising a child alone, or commuting three hours a day to a deeply unsatisfying cubicle job, or doing laundry in a nursing home, or running a hospital ward, or being a luggage handler, or digging septic systems, or waiting tables at a delicatessen, or—for that matter—pretty much anything else that people do?"

She has a point, I'll admit; for the right kind of personality, writing is "the best life there is, because you get to live within the realm of your own mind, and that is a profoundly rare human privilege." And yet, what Gilbert overlooks is that, in a field whose rewards are often fleeting, part of the fun lies in grumbling about how difficult it is.

Roth, who announced his retirement shortly after his encounter with Tepper, recently described the process this way: "You build a book out of sentences. And the sentences are built up out of details. So you're working brick by brick. And the bricks are heavy." Gilbert herself cites Balzac ("I am a galley slave to pen and ink"), William Styron ("Let's face it. Writing is hell") and Norman Mailer ("Every one of my books killed me a little more"). And they're not the only ones.

For years, I've found solace in *The Writer's Quotation Book*, edited by James Charlton, a slight compendium of quotes about the writing life. There are all the usual noble sentiments about literature and how it enlarges us, but the best stuff, by far, are the complaints.

Here's Red Smith: "There's nothing to writing. All you do is sit down at a typewriter and open a vein." Or Georges Simenon: "Writing is not a profession but a vocation of unhappiness."

Peter de Vries insists, "I love being a writer. What I can't stand is the paperwork." And then, of course, there's Hemingway: "They can't yank a novelist like they can a pitcher. A novelist has to go the full nine even if it kills him."

This, I think, is what Roth was saying, that it's tough to have to go the full nine every time. In that sense, his comments are more encouragement than admonition, which Tepper seems to understand as well. In his *The Paris Review* post, he ponders what he should have said, and finally settles on the key faith of the writer, the thing that makes all the work, the struggle, worthwhile.

"I still feel strongly," Tepper writes, "that the one thing a writer has above all else, the reward which is bigger than anything that may come to him … is the weapon against boredom. The question of how to spend his time, what to do today, tomorrow, and during all the other pockets of time in between when some doing is required: this is not applicable to the writer. For he can always lose himself in the act of writing and make time vanish. After which, he actually has something to show for his efforts. Not bad."